Kung Fu Princess 3
Veil of Secrets

Written by Pamela Walker

Grosset & Dunlap
A Parachute Press Book

ഗ ഗ ഗ ഗ ഗ

GROSSET & DUNLAP
Published by the Penguin Group
Penguin Group (USA) Inc., 375 Hudson Street, New York, New York 10014, U.S.A.
Penguin Group (Canada), 90 Eglinton Avenue East, Suite 700, Toronto, Ontario,
Canada M4P 2Y3 (a division of Pearson Penguin Canada Inc.)
Penguin Books Ltd, 80 Strand, London WC2R 0RL, England
Penguin Ireland, 25 St Stephen's Green, Dublin 2, Ireland
(a division of Penguin Books Ltd)
Penguin Group (Australia), 250 Camberwell Road, Camberwell, Victoria 3124,
Australia
(a division of Pearson Australia Group Pty Ltd)
Penguin Books India Pvt Ltd, 11 Community Centre, Panchsheel Park, New Delhi
- 110 017, India
Penguin Group (NZ), Cnr Airborne and Rosedale Roads, Albany, Auckland 1310,
New Zealand
(a division of Pearson New Zealand Ltd)
Penguin Books (South Africa) (Pty) Ltd, 24 Sturdee Avenue, Rosebank,
Johannesburg 2196, South Africa

Penguin Books Ltd, Registered Offices:
80 Strand, London WC2R 0RL, England

Cover photograph by David Mager/Pearson Learning Group

Library of Congress Cataloging-in-Publication Data is available.

ISBN 0-448-44141-1   10 9 8 7 6 5 4 3 2 1

99614

KUNG FU PRINCESS 3

The Prophecy

A daughter of light,
Blood of Ng Mui and Yim Wing Chun,
Will be born into the power of her ancestors,
Born to finish the battles they began.
In her fourteenth year her destiny will unfold:
Through five gold coins, each death or strength.
Her ancestors' enemies will seek her,
The demons and ghosts will gather,
But in gold and jade, she will find her gifts,
And the veil of secrets will open to her.

 Prologue

On Cassidy Chen's fourteenth birthday, a mysterious man gave her a gift of five Chinese coins and an ancient prophecy began to unfold. That night Cassidy dreamed of her Chinese ancestors Ng Mui and Wing Chun, two women warriors who called her Mingmei and told her that she was destined to be a warrior princess.

Five evil spirits, imprisoned in the ancient coins for over three hundred years, had now been released and wanted revenge. *As you are of our blood, Mingmei, they will try to destroy you*, her ancestors warned.

When Cassidy became the victim of bizarre

accidents and an unexplainable illness, she suspected a connection to the coins. On a night when Cassidy was at her weakest, she came face-to-face with a demon — a deadly flying snake! After a terrifying battle Cassidy defeated the snake demon. In exchange she received a gift from the spirits of her ancestors — *the ability to heal quickly.*

The second demon was a plague ghost that brought torrential rain, wind, and unrelenting thunderstorms to Seattle. Cassidy defeated the ancient demon using skills learned from Master Lau, her Wing Chun kung fu teacher. For defeating the plague ghost, Cassidy earned *the gift of seeing spirits.*

Cassidy soon discovered the image on the third coin represented a trickster demon, half fox and half man. After battling the demon's illusions Cassidy received *the gift of heightened senses.*

With help from her friend James, Cassidy learned that the fourth demon was within her! This powerful enemy was formed from Cassidy's dark thoughts and negative emotions — anger, jealousy, and fear. In a spectacular sword fight, Cassidy defeated the demon by facing the worst qualities in herself. The gift from her ancestors this time was the *calm mind of a warrior.*

Cassidy decided that the time had come to tell Master Lau about all the things that had happened to her since receiving the coins. Her parents would never believe her, but perhaps *he* could help. But when she visited his office, she witnessed a terrifying ritual—Master Lau was calling forth sinister spirits.

Feeling frightened and alone, Cassidy decided to give up. She just couldn't fight anymore. It was too much.

But then she remembered her gift, her calm warrior mind. She could control her dark fears. As Cassidy realized this, she saw a vision of her future self in the mirror—a beautiful and strong woman dressed in a robe of gold and jade. The woman's words astonished her: *You are not alone. Your grandfather is alive!*

Now Cassidy knew that she would never give up. She felt certain that her grandfather was the key to understanding her destiny. She hoped to find him when she visited Hong Kong for a Wing Chun tournament in August.

In the meantime, she trained in secret so that Master Lau wouldn't discover how powerful she was becoming. Her true teachers now were her ancient ancestors whose words echoed in her head and heart. She had to be ready for whatever the fifth coin would bring.

One final coin remains, and the story continues . . .

 # Chapter One

The purple and gold sign read *Your Destiny—Unveiled! Madame Zona Knows All, Sees All!* At the moment that Cassidy Chen looked up at the sign, three long icicles fell and then shattered on the sidewalk at her feet. The sound was like breaking glass as the icicles skittered across the slick sidewalk like diamonds thrown from above.

"Did you know that people have actually been killed by falling icicles?" her best friend, Eliza Clifford, said. "I saw a TV special about it once."

"No, I didn't know that," Cassidy said, stepping

into the open doorway before she met a similar fate. She'd had more than her fair share of danger lately.

The two girls had spent the afternoon shopping for new clothes. Fourteen-year-old Cassidy had grown taller and slimmer since her birthday in September. Now, at the end of April, she needed new jeans that actually covered the tops of her shoes instead of striking her midankle.

"This is some freaky weather, huh?" Eliza said, following Cassidy into the warm shop. "It feels more like January than late April."

"A little too freaky," Cassidy commented, peering up at the steel-colored sky. The strange weather probably had a completely logical cause, but she couldn't be sure. Not after all of her bizarre experiences with demons.

Eliza gave Cassidy a wary look. "You don't think . . ." She shook her head. "Forget it. So what is this place?" She turned to check out their surroundings, abruptly changing the subject.

Cassidy and Eliza had been best friends for practically forever, but the day that Cassidy told Eliza about the demons, their friendship started to change. Eliza couldn't understand why Cassidy wouldn't just make it all stop. Then, after Eliza had been attacked and poisoned by the fox demon, she had been really angry that Cassidy didn't get rid of the coins once and for all. They didn't speak for a while, and only started hanging out together again pretty recently. But Cassidy knew that she could no longer confide in her best friend—Eliza just didn't want to hear about anything having to do with the demons. Besides, Cassidy felt the less Eliza knew, the safer her friend would be.

"This is a wacky-looking place," Eliza said.

Cassidy scanned the room. A long glass case ran the length of the store on one side from front to back. Inside the case Cassidy saw a tray of silver charms on silk cords. There was also a box filled with what looked like gnarled roots. Another tray contained small vials of liquid in the colors of amber, sapphire, and emerald. The large glass jars on the shelves near the door held dried powders and curls of tiny leaves and seedpods.

Cassidy pointed at a sign on the back wall. "Madame Zona knows all!" she read aloud. "This must be some kind of fortune-teller's shop."

"Hilarious," Eliza said. "Check out the crystal ball. Oh, and look at this card!" She picked up a dark blue business card covered in stars and planets from a stack on the counter. "No appointment necessary," she read. "I know when you're coming!" She laughed as she put the card back. "So cheesy."

"There you are!" a large woman said as she came into the shop from a curtained room in the back.

"I've been expecting you." She wore a flowing purple caftan printed with small yellow lightning bolts. Her face was as round as the moon, and her silvery white hair hung in one long braid down her back.

Eliza smirked at Cassidy. Her look said, *This is gonna be good!* "You were expecting us?" she asked.

"Of course! Madame Zona knows all." The woman gestured as if she were embracing the entire universe. "So who will be first?" Madame Zona asked. "You're here for a reading, right? You want to know about your future?"

"You really think a woman who calls herself Madame Zona is gonna tell me something about my destiny?" Cassidy whispered to Eliza. "I think I already know more than I need to know."

"Excuse us," Eliza said to Madame Zona. She grabbed Cassidy's arm and turned her around so that they faced away from Madame Zona.

"Come on, Cass," Eliza whispered. "It'll be fun! Let's see what crazy stuff she tells us!"

Fun. Cassidy craved regular, ordinary, eighth-grade fun. Especially since she felt in her very bones that the next demon could be waiting for her around the corner. There was still one coin left whose demon hadn't been revealed to her yet, and she had no idea what to expect.

The strange engraving on the fifth coin haunted Cassidy's every thought: The outer edge was ringed with faces—their mouths open in what looked like agonized moans or terrified screams.

She doubted Madame Zona would actually tell her anything useful, but then again, she wasn't there for useful. She was there for fun.

"Okay," Cassidy said, shaking off the creepy image of the coin. She looked at Eliza's grinning face. "Let's do it!"

"We're in!" Eliza declared as they turned back around.

"Of course you are," Madame Zona said. "I knew that." Madame Zona's voice was melodic, hypnotic almost. It wasn't so much her accent— French, maybe, Cassidy thought—but it was the way her words trilled out of her mouth like a song. The woman was totally dramatic and over-the-top, but also totally mesmerizing.

"You are first." She pointed a long finger at Eliza. "I do my spiritual readings back here."

She motioned for Eliza to follow her through the curtain. Cassidy watched the woman's long braid swinging back and forth along her back like a silver pendulum as she exited the room.

While Eliza was with Madame Zona, Cassidy explored the shop. She wondered if maybe there was something in one of the books for sale that might tell her about the image on the fifth coin. She was flipping through a third one when the curtains parted.

"Your turn!" Madame Zona sang out as Eliza came back into the shop grinning broadly.

"Go for it," Eliza urged.

 Chapter Two

Cassidy followed Madame Zona into a small room lit with several candles. They sat across from each other at a round table covered with a white cloth.

Madame Zona took a small bundle from one of her pockets and untied a lavender scarf. Inside was a deck of cards.

"Please hold these for a moment," she said. Cassidy took the stack of cards and held them in her hand. Now that she was up close, Cassidy could see that the woman had one brown eye and one blue eye. "The tarot cards are reading your energy—your heart," Madame Zona said before taking them from Cassidy.

"Now, let's see what we have." Madame Zona shuffled the deck and instructed Cassidy to cut the cards. Quickly Madame Zona turned four of the cards face up in a diamond pattern in front of her.

"We see your past—your present—your . . ." Madame Zona began.

"My future?" Cassidy offered, wondering why the psychic stopped midsentence.

"We shall start over," Madame Zona said, and quickly repeated the entire procedure. This time, she studied the four cards and then looked deeply into Cassidy's eyes.

"Your past has been filled with battles," Madame Zona said quietly, almost whispering. Cassidy had to lean in closer to hear her.

Battles, Cassidy thought. *Does she see . . . ? No, she must mean something more general. What teen isn't faced with some kind of battles, like fights with parents, friends, trouble at school? I'm sure she doesn't mean the kind of battles that I've been—*

"A snake with wings. I see *poison!*"

Cassidy swallowed hard, and her face flushed. *Is she actually seeing what happened?*

"And I see water. A deadly surge of water!" Madame Zona's voice was breathy and monotone, as if she were in a trance. Her words seared Cassidy with the accuracy of what she was saying—and seeing!

"Next, I see a creature. Half man, half *fox*!" Madame Zona said. She held her large hand over the cards, but she looked directly at Cassidy, her eyes blinking in disbelief at what she was saying, as if she had no control over the words that were coming out of her mouth.

Cassidy wanted to run from the room. She felt exposed sitting there while this woman peered into her past and saw all the unbelievable things that had been happening to her all these months. But she couldn't move—she *had* to know the rest. She hoped Madame Zona would be able to tell her what kind of demon she would have to fight next. *But do I even want to know?*

"And then . . ." Madame Zona closed her eyes for a moment before continuing. "You fought . . . *yourself*!" She hissed the last word.

"But how could you . . .?" Cassidy began. She felt sick, and the room seemed to be closing in on her. "How do you know all this?"

"It is in the cards, dear," Madame Zona said. "The past, the present, the . . ."

Cassidy waited for her to go on. The woman sat perfectly still and closed her eyes again, as if she might be actually witnessing the battles behind her lids. Her eyes fluttered for a moment and then opened. She peered deeply into Cassidy's jade green eyes, and Cassidy found that she couldn't look away from the woman with one blue and one brown eye. Eyes that were wide with astonishment and fear.

She saw something, Cassidy realized. Something that disturbed her, that frightened her beyond belief. The urge to run was almost overwhelming — to get out of the small, hot room with its flickering candles and dark, mysterious cards spread on the table. But she had to find out what the woman was holding back. "What is it?" Cassidy asked. "What is it you're not telling me?"

Madame Zona gazed down at the cards and then back up at Cassidy. She took a deep breath and leaned in closer. She placed her large, manicured hand over Cassidy's smaller one. "Your future . . . it is . . . *uncertain*," Madame Zona said at last.

❀ Chapter Three

"Uncertain?" Cassidy repeated. "What are you talking about?" She knew she was almost shouting, but she didn't care. "What do you *see*?"

"This has never happened to me before," Madame Zona said. She quickly gathered the cards together, tied them back into the lavender scarf, and returned them to her pocket. She stood up, and Cassidy knew that she wanted her to leave. Immediately.

"You have to tell me what you're talking about," Cassidy pleaded. "You can't say that my future is *uncertain* and then expect me to just go! What did you see in the cards?"

"That's just it! I don't see anything!" Madame Zona sat down heavily in the chair, causing the round table to shake.

Cassidy was beyond freaked out now. This was supposed to be fun! A goof! The psychic was supposed to tell her that a boyfriend was in her future—maybe, *hopefully*, James Tang. And that she would do well at the Wing Chun tournament in Hong Kong in August. But instead she was hearing that her future was *not there*! Cassidy willed herself to be calm. She had to find out what this woman knew, and it wouldn't do any good if she got upset or angry. *The calm mind of a warrior*, Cassidy reminded herself, and pictured the cool, still water of a pool.

Madame Zona looked absolutely wiped out. Her large, round face was beaded with perspiration, and she mopped at it with a green handkerchief that she had taken from another pocket.

"I really need to know what you saw," Cassidy said quietly but firmly, even though her heart felt as if it might beat out of her chest. "I know that you aren't telling me everything."

The woman dropped her hands to her lap and sighed. "When I read someone's future," she explained, "I usually see something—some little thing—that gives me a clue, and from that I make a prediction. For instance, I might see a plane taking off and the prediction might be that someone would soon be leaving on a trip."

"I understand," Cassidy said. "But for me you said that you saw *nothing*? Not one clue?"

"With you there's . . ." Madame Zona seemed to be struggling to find the best way to describe what she saw—or didn't see. "It's as if there's a fog—or perhaps a curtain or veil—that covers your future, and I can't see past it."

The confusing words settled heavily on Cassidy. What did Madame Zona mean? And why was this curtain, or whatever it was, there at all?

Then Cassidy had an even more disturbing question. The fifth coin—why couldn't Madame Zona see what she was going to have to fight next? She had seen the four demons of the past, so why couldn't she see the fifth one? Cassidy shuddered. *Is it going to be so bad this time that I might not . . .*

"Are you sure that's all you saw? Just this . . . veil?" Cassidy asked. She wondered if her voice sounded as weak to Madame Zona as it did to her own ears. "You've told me everything?"

"I'm afraid so, dear." Madame Zona leaned across the table again, and Cassidy shivered, seeing the exhaustion and utter fear in the woman's brown and blue eyes. "I'm afraid you're involved in something that is quite dangerous," she whispered. "My advice to you is to walk away from whatever you've gotten yourself mixed up in."

Walk away, Cassidy thought. *How do you walk away from your life?* She could never explain to Madame Zona why that wasn't possible. Cassidy stood, and her legs felt weak and unsteady. "I need to go now," she said, worried that if she didn't get out of the small, hot room she might faint. "I need some fresh air."

Back on the sidewalk Eliza was bubbling over with Madame Zona's news. "She said there's a *farmer* in my future. I think she means Ben Aronson," Eliza said. "Remember, Ben was dressed like the straw man from the *Wizard of Oz* at the Halloween party?"

"But the straw man wasn't a farmer," Cassidy pointed out as they got on the bus to go back home.

"No, but there's still a connection. Remember, he was a straw man in Oz. But when he was in Kansas, he worked on the *farm*," Eliza said. "Besides, Ben has e-mailed me a couple of times, and I really think he likes me."

"That's great, Eliza," Cassidy said, her stomach churning as the bus lurched forward from stop to stop. *Madame Zona sees a cute guy from Wilder High in Eliza's future and she sees* nothing *in mine!*

"So what did Madame Zona tell you? Is James going to get a clue and dump Majesta for you?"

"Not . . . not exactly."

Eliza's cheerful expression vanished as she

studied Cassidy's face. "She saw something about the coins, didn't she?"

"Sort of," Cassidy admitted.

Eliza sighed and stared out the bus window. It was obvious she didn't want to talk about it.

Cassidy tried to visualize a still, clear pool, in order to keep the calm mind of a warrior. But with Madame Zona's ominous words still hissing in her head, it was hard to do. Instead Cassidy wondered what was so horrifying in her future that it was hidden behind a heavy veil.

🌸 *Chapter Four*

The following week, twelve students in Master Lau's Wing Chun class stood waiting for the *shifu*. Cassidy dreaded coming to the classes ever since the evening two months ago when she had secretly witnessed her teacher's sinister ceremony. But she knew she needed to keep coming. She didn't want to raise Master Lau's suspicion that she knew his secret. Besides, despite everything, he was still an amazing teacher. She needed all the knowledge and skill he could impart.

"Hey, I finally had my first private class with

Master Lau," Luis whispered. Luis Alvarez was one of Cassidy's best friends in Wing Chun, and he would be going to Hong Kong in August with Cassidy, along with Majesta Madison and James Tang. "It was *intense*," Luis said. "Master Lau is an awesome teacher. We're really lucky, Cass, you know?"

"Yeah, I know, Luis," Cassidy said. There was no way she could tell Luis that she saw Master Lau conjuring dark spirits in his office. One thing that Cassidy had decided was that the fewer people who knew about the ancient coins and the demons, the better.

Cassidy glanced across the room at James Tang. James knew everything. Well—everything except what Cassidy had seen Master Lau doing. She planned on bringing him to Ethos Café and telling him right after class today.

She hadn't spent any time alone with James for a while. It was just too hard to face him ever since the day she had fought the fourth demon—her dark half. The demon had told James Cassidy's true feelings about him. Cassidy still cringed as she remembered the girl's words: *I've been crushing on you since the first day I saw you, James.*

In the past couple of months, James had seemed kind of uncomfortable with Cassidy, too. Besides, she thought with a pang, he seemed to be spending most of his free time with the gorgeous, perfect Majesta.

Things have to get normal between us, Cassidy vowed. She had suspected for a while that James was the ally that her Chinese ancestors had promised her. He'd had her back almost since the day the coins first started unleashing their power against Cassidy. He had provided the antique sword that she used to kill the winged snake demon. He'd helped her try to understand the mythology behind the coins, thanks to his father's extensive library and his early years in Hong Kong. He'd even been the one to figure out that the fourth demon liked to act out on Cassidy's negative emotions. Then he helped Cassidy trap the demon. Cassidy needed him. But did that make him her ally? Or was it just wishful thinking because she had a major crush on him?

Master Lau walked out of his office and crossed the floor to face his students. Cassidy bowed to show respect as the other students did, but in her heart she had only contempt for the man. Clearly he was involved in something very bad—something that very likely involved her.

"We shall begin with *chi sau*," Master Lau said as he began pairing off students. "One cannot win a battle unless one knows his opponent's moves *before* his opponent even makes a move."

Cassidy shook her head slightly to let go of the thoughts that were diverting her attention away from the drills. She and Luis were paired together for sticking hands practice, and she tried to stay focused on what she was doing. They faced each other, wrists to elbows, no more than a breath apart as they circled each other, anticipating each move. Cassidy made a slow move to the right, and Luis was right there. She made a slight move to the left and then back to the right, and once again Luis kept up with her.

"Luis, you're really good at this," she said as Luis blocked her from completing a wrist hold.

Luis grinned, his brown eyes twinkling. "I've been practicing. I can't let you and James show me up in Hong Kong. I have to hold my own!"

Cassidy glanced across the gym and noticed that James and Majesta had also been paired. Despite having learned to be better at controlling her emotions, Cassidy felt the familiar stab of jealousy. Majesta had always seemed so perfectly put together, and she always seemed to get whatever she wanted — including James.

Dark thoughts are dangerous, she reminded herself. She forced herself to look away from Majesta and James.

❧ *Chapter Five*

"Let's now move into position for instruction," Master Lau said. His voice sounded cold and hollow to Cassidy.

The students ended their sticking hands drills and began moving apart and standing at attention in preparation for their teacher's lesson. Cassidy saw that James had found a position near her along the back of the group. She looked over at him and gave him a quick smile, and practically melted when he did the same.

"Let's talk about weapons for a moment,"

Master Lau began, and looked out over the students, who listened intently. "What weapons do you think of in traditional kung fu warfare?"

Luis's hand immediately shot up. "Swords, spears," he said when Master Lau called on him. "Oh, yeah, halberds!"

Cassidy thought about the antique *nandao*, or broadsword, that she used to kill the snake demon.

"Correct, Luis," Master Lau said, and he walked over to a nearby wall and removed one of the padded instructional swords. "There was a time in certain Chinese dynasties when it was forbidden to own weapons of any kind. Traditional weapons of warfare — such as the sword, spear, or halberd — were confiscated, and the owner of the forbidden weapon might even be executed."

"Whoa!" said Luis softly.

"Warriors learned to be very clever," Master Lau said as he returned the instructional sword to its place on the pegged board. Cassidy frowned as she saw him reach up and take down another weapon from the board. It was one she'd never seen before, but from the glint along its curved edge, it was clear that the weapon was very sharp. "This is a sickle," he said. "Farmers used these tools to cut weeds from their crops and also to clear heavy brush along the roadside." He ran his finger along the outside edge of the curved blade. "The farmer would sharpen the interior edge of the blade, and with a sweeping motion he would cut the offending weeds." Master Lau then lowered the sickle and demonstrated how a farmer might walk along swinging the sickle back and forth.

"Imagine how common it would be to see a village farmer with his sickle, clearing his property of overgrown weeds and small trees," he said, walking now along the perimeter of the students. "There would be absolutely nothing out of the ordinary, and the authorities would pass him right by as he toiled in the sun without giving him a second thought." *What's he up to?* Cassidy wondered.

"Now imagine this same sickle," he said. "Just a simple farmer's tool in the hands of a trained warrior!" In an almost blinding flash of dark cloth and metal weapon, Master Lau quickly turned, brandished the sickle above his head, and then sliced through the air between Cassidy and James. The curved blade created a metallic whir as it tore past them. Cassidy was too stunned at first to even register what had just happened. She glanced at James, who looked shaken but stared straight ahead.

And then there was silence as everyone held their breath in awe of what they had just seen. Master Lau stepped back, held the sickle across both hands, and looked at his students. Cassidy noticed that he was avoiding looking at her or James.

Cassidy's heart was pounding. *Is he trying to intimidate us?* she wondered. *Is he trying to prove something?*

Finally, with a small nod Master Lau walked back toward the front of the group and returned the sickle to one of the hooks on the board. He took down several of the instructional swords and began distributing them to his students along with mandatory chest pads. "Now, as we practice our sword drills today, let's imagine fighting in the tradition of the ancient warrior," Master Lau said as he tossed one of the padded swords to Cassidy, who caught it by the handle. "Just for today, try to imagine that this isn't an instructional sword padded for safety—but something much more deadly!"

ꙅꙅꙅꙅꙅ

"So, what's up, Crane Girl?" James said as he placed two steaming mugs of caramel macchiato on the table at Ethos Café after Wing Chun class. "Besides Lau's crazy quotient, I mean." He slid into the seat opposite Cassidy, his expression friendly but guarded. It had been a long time since they'd been alone together, and he looked uncomfortable.

"Yeah, was that whole farmer's sickle thing weird, or what?" Cassidy said.

"I think he's totally out of his mind," James said.

Cassidy took a small careful sip and then looked up at James. "Actually, Master Lau is what I wanted to talk to you about," she blurted out. She didn't want him to think the reason she asked to see him was, well, *personal.* "I saw him doing something really bizarre in his office. Something dangerous."

James's brown eyes grew intense as Cassidy told him what she'd seen. He stopped her a couple of times to ask questions, but mostly he just listened. It was a relief to get it all out.

"It was so evil, James," Cassidy said. "The spirits were dark, and they looked *tormented* or something. It was kind of like he was calling them out."

"Yeah," James said. "But out of *where*? And *why*?"

Cassidy felt gratitude in every cell of her body. James didn't doubt anything she'd said. He accepted the weird stories, the bizarre things that had happened to her, and he tried—really *tried*—to help her find the answers.

James leaned across the table toward her, and Cassidy noticed a shadow cross his dark eyes. "I think this is way beyond dangerous, Cassidy," he said. "I'm really worried about you. I mean, I know you can fight—I still can't believe how you destroyed that . . . well, your dark side that day on the lake."

Please, please, Cassidy thought, *let's not talk about that day!* She was relieved when James didn't go there. Instead he said, "Cassidy, somehow Master Lau's mixed up in this whole ancient coin thing, the demons, all of it, right?"

"I think so," Cassidy said.

"Why didn't you tell me right away?" James asked.

"I . . . uh . . . I . . ." Could she admit she'd felt too embarrassed to talk to him? He knew all about her jealousy, her crush on him. She just shrugged.

"This must be tough for you," he said, glancing down at his mug, deftly avoiding looking at Cassidy. "I know how much you respected Master Lau." Cassidy nodded, relieved that James was just as determined to avoid talking about "the incident" as she was.

"Yeah, it was a shock," she admitted. "I didn't want to believe it. I think he wants the coins—and somehow it seems to be tied up with my grandfather."

"Maybe he wants to use the power in the coins—to do evil, or control people, or something," James said.

Cassidy thought about that. "Right. I mean, I know there's some kind of power in owning the coins," she said. "Like I know I've become stronger at Wing Chun. Plus, there are the gifts from the ancestors each time I defeat one of the demons. But if he can't take the coins," Cassidy said, "and I have no intention of giving them to him, then how do you think he plans on getting them?"

James took a long sip from his mug and set it down on the table before answering. "I don't think you want to hear this, but I think the dark spirits you saw in his office are part of his plan."

Chapter Six

That night, shaken by James's words, Cassidy opened the warrior's shrine on her nightstand and touched the delicate pattern of jade leaves and gold vines. Just looking at the beautiful strong wood and the intricate design made Cassidy feel close to her ancestors. "I need help," Cassidy whispered softly. "There's something bad ahead, and I don't know what to do. I don't know how to prepare . . ."

Cassidy's ancestors had told her that she was a warrior—but she didn't feel very much like one now. She felt like a very frightened fourteen-year-old girl who was in over her head.

She took out the fifth coin from the carved box and looked at the engraving. Those openmouthed faces carved in a ring around the coin sent a shiver along her spine. They looked tormented, hungry, screaming, moaning, more frightening than anything she'd seen before. Her hands trembled as she put the coin back in the box.

What kind of demon will I have to fight next? She knew the faces on the coin somehow indicated her next foe. She needed to know that her ancestors were with her — she needed their guidance.

Cassidy closed her eyes in quiet meditation, her breath slow and even, and concentrated all her attention on her great-grandmother Fiona.

When Cassidy opened her eyes, the spirit of Fiona stood before her. Her shimmering green dress and fiery red hair filled Cassidy's room with warmth and color — but there was something different about the beautiful woman this time. Green eyes that had twinkled before looked serious now. *Serious and very concerned*, Cassidy realized with a dark foreboding.

"*My darling*," her great-grandmother said. "*You have so many questions. Please believe that the answers are coming—in time.*"

"In *time*," Cassidy repeated, and she felt a catch in her throat. "But it's just that I feel . . ." Cassidy began, her throat tightening at what she was about to confess, "that I *don't* have much time."

In a rush of emotion, the words spilled out. She told her great-grandmother about Madame Zona's vision of her future—that the psychic could see nothing there because it was hidden behind a veil. And how the image on the fifth coin disturbed her thoughts every waking hour.

Cassidy hoped that Fiona would laugh and tell her how wrong she was—that she had nothing to worry about. But instead her great-grandmother lowered her jade green eyes and seemed to be searching for the right words to say. At last she looked up at Cassidy.

"*Beautiful daughter,*" her great-grandmother's spirit said, "*your future is out there, but I'm afraid this woman was correct. It is hidden by a darkness that only you can lift—that you* must *lift!*"

"The fifth coin," Cassidy said. "Is the darkness caused by the fifth coin?"

"*I'm afraid so. The only way your future can be secured so that you can fulfill your destiny is to defeat this darkness. Lift the heavy veil that threatens the spirits of your ancestors.*"

"But I don't understand!" Cassidy cried, her voice trembling with the sick fear of not knowing what was to come. She needed answers—but Cassidy could already see the image of her Irish ancestor beginning to change. "Please don't go. I need help!" she pleaded.

The rich colors shimmered and faded into a

pale watery image just before disappearing altogether. Even though she could no longer be seen, Great-grandmother Fiona's disembodied voice chilled Cassidy to the bone: *"Unless you save us, our spirits will be devoured, my darling one. It will be as if we never lived. And if we cease to exist, then there can be no you. It will be as if you had never lived!"*

🌸 *Chapter Seven*

"Cassidy, didn't you hear your father?" Wendy Chen asked at dinnertime.

"Oh, sorry, Dad," Cassidy said. "I guess I zoned out." Cassidy looked down at her plate and saw that she hadn't eaten a thing. She had been replaying last night's visit from her great-grandmother over and over in her head, wondering what she had meant when she said, "our spirits will be devoured." *So creepy!*

"I *said* I've decided to go to Hong Kong with you in August," Simon told her. "I've got cousins there who I haven't seen in years, and it will be nice to reconnect. I want them to meet you. They're your family."

"That's great, Dad," Cassidy exclaimed. But instantly her excitement turned to worry. *What if something happens to Dad in Hong Kong—because of me?* It was already May. Less than three months before the Wing Chun tournament, and she still had no idea what to expect from the fifth coin or when the demon would strike.

She had also hoped the trip would be an opportunity to get to know James better, and she certainly didn't want a chaperone for that.

"What about you, Mom?" Cassidy asked. "Is this gonna be a family trip?" Maybe if both of her parents came, they'd hang out together—away from her and James, and away from potential danger.

"I'm afraid not," Wendy answered. "August is when everybody wants to take off, and I've got too many vacations to cover at the preschool."

"That's too bad," Cassidy said. "I wish you could go."

"Me too, but you're going to be busy preparing for the tournament, being with your friends," her mom said. "And in case you're worried that your Dad will expect you to spend every minute with him, I've made him promise to give you some time for yourself."

Cassidy laughed—her mother knew her so well! "Thanks, Mom," she said. "But Dad, I *would* like to meet my cousins—and I'm really glad you're going."

"I'm happy to hear you say that, Cass," her father said. "I've been working on the family history."

"He's even made a chart," Cassidy's mother added. "A very *big* family chart."

"That's cool, Dad," Cassidy said. "I'd like to see it."

After dinner Cassidy followed her father back to his office. Along one wall Simon had a long paper chart that showed several generations of the Chen family. There were small photos pasted next to some of the names on the chart.

"This is your grandfather, my father, Li Chen," Simon told her as he pointed to the name. Cassidy looked at the small photo, the white streak against the young man's dark hair.

Just like the man who gave me the coins, Cassidy thought to herself. After the vision of her future self told her that her grandfather was alive, she had thought about telling her father. She knew he would want to know. But how *could* she? She'd have to tell him that she'd been seeing visions and that the spirits of her dead ancestors were talking to her! He'd never believe her.

She studied the photo on the chart. *If my grandfather really is alive, then I have to trust that he'll let us know when the time is right.*

"Cassidy, did I ever tell you that my mother always believed my father was watching over us from beyond?" Simon asked.

"No, Dad," Cassidy said, wondering where he was going with this. Did he suspect something?

"My mother would often find white feathers on her walks to the store or to school with me. She'd pick up the feather and say, 'See, Simon, this is a sign that your father is still with us.'"

"Why white feathers?" Cassidy asked.

"I think there was some family legend about the Chens being watched over by a white crane. Sort of a guardian angel thing."

"Interesting . . ." Cassidy remembered how well she had been able to learn the crane stance, and how much she loved it when James called her Crane Girl. "When your mother told you that the feathers meant your father was looking out for you, did you believe her?" Cassidy asked him.

Simon smiled. "As a child, yes. It was very comforting to think that he was still around. Even now, if I happen to see a feather on the ground, it makes me think about him. It's kind of nice."

"Yeah, it *is* nice," Cassidy said as she studied the photo of the young man who was her grandfather.

Maybe he is *watching out for us,* she thought.

"As you can see, I still have a ways to go," Simon told her as he pointed out several blank lines on the family chart. "I'm hoping to get more of our family history when I visit my cousins in Hong Kong."

Suddenly Cassidy threw her arms around her dad and hugged him tight. "I'm really glad you're going," she said.

"Me too." Simon gave her a kiss on the top of her head as she released him.

She had no idea what would happen in Hong Kong, but she had to admit that it would be good to have her dad along. *If I even make it to Hong Kong,* she worried, feeling a chill run along the nape of her neck. *The demon from the fifth coin may come after me before August.*

James had promised her that when they got to Hong Kong, they could do more research to try to learn what the coins were all about. But Cassidy couldn't shake the feeling that time was running out. She remembered the words of her great-grandmother Fiona: *Unless you save us, our spirits will be devoured.* What would it be like to cease to exist—to simply, suddenly be *no more?*

A wave of cold air washed over her, chilling her to the bone. She glanced at the windows along the back wall expecting to see them open, but they were closed and the curtains hung still. There was a crackle of paper as the family chart separated from the wall and fell. Cassidy's family history, so carefully prepared by her father, dropped to the floor in a long, twisted curl of paper that landed at her feet.

 Chapter Eight

Cassidy was jittery all week, but to her enormous relief, nothing strange happened. No demons, no spirits, just normal end-of-the-school-year stuff.

After Wednesday's Wing Chun class Master Lau gave Cassidy, James, Majesta, and Luis a list of sightseeing opportunities and events that would be taking place during their August trip to Hong Kong.

This is really happening, Cassidy thought, gazing down at a photo of a dragon costume.

"This trip is gonna be so awesome," Luis said, poring over his info packet.

"There are serious places to shop in Hong Kong," Majesta said. "I wonder if there are any outlet stores there."

Cassidy noticed that James just stuffed his papers in his backpack. "Gotta go," he said. Cassidy watched in dismay as James and Majesta headed out together.

"Cool!" Luis exclaimed. "It looks like we'll be there during this Hungry Ghost Festival thing. That sounds like fun, huh?"

"Festival of Hungry Ghosts?" Cassidy repeated. "What's that?"

"Like a street festival, I think," Luis said, peering at the tourist pack. "Or maybe like Halloween—or sort of a combination of both."

"Sounds amazing," Cassidy said. "I love street festivals *and* Halloween."

"Yeah, creepy and fun," Luis said. "It says that people set up altars with food and incense for the 'hungry ghosts,' and there's music and dancing in the streets and then a big bonfire at the end."

Cassidy pictured a roaring bonfire and the swirling dark ghosts in the smoke. The image wavered for a moment in her head and then was replaced by a more disturbing one: Master Lau dripping oil onto a burning candle, dark spirits rising out of the flame.

"You okay?" Luis asked. "You zone out or something?"

"Uh, yeah, I'm okay," Cassidy said, shaking away the terrifying image. But she couldn't shake away the dread that something bad would happen there and that Master Lau would be deeply involved.

ᘯ ᘯ ᘯ ᘯ ᘯ

Friday evening while Cassidy waited to begin her private lesson with Master Lau, she wished again that she could have canceled. Ever since she discovered he was dealing with dark spirits she'd been nervous about being alone with him. But good judgment told her that ditching the session would have been a bad idea. He might have called her parents, and then she would have had to figure out a way to explain her absence to them. As much as she dreaded being alone with the *shifu*, she didn't want to arouse any suspicions about how much she knew.

When the door to his office opened and he walked across the floor to join her, her body tensed. *Calm down*, she ordered herself. *You can do this. You have to do this!*

"The most profound and mysterious aspect of kung fu is the power of chi," Master Lau said. "Do you understand chi, Cassidy?"

"It's like a force or energy inside each of us," Cassidy replied.

"Yes, it is that and more," the *shifu* said. "Chi

can be controlled, its power harnessed—and *used.*"

For the next thirty minutes Master Lau led Cassidy through a series of exercises he said would help her develop strong chi that she could direct when fighting.

Cassidy concentrated on her breathing, feeling the flow of chi from her abdomen as she punched, blocked, and kicked. She used her forearm to slice the air, effectively stopping Master Lau's strike. Her adrenaline pumped as she went on the aggressive with a right twist, elbow block, and high left kick. The words *fight, fight, fight* coursed through her head as she single-mindedly moved forward, backing the *shifu* toward the wall. *I can take him down!* she thought.

Master Lau stopped and faced Cassidy. The look on his face was one of surprise. *And,* Cassidy realized, *can that be fear?*

He cleared his throat before speaking. "You have much power, Cassidy. Your focus and concentration are to be admired."

"Thank you, *Shifu,*" Cassidy said. Her heart felt heavy at hearing her teacher's praise. It always used to make her day to receive any kind of compliment from Master Lau, but now there was so much confusion and doubt about who he really was that his words were meaningless.

"It is a good feeling to be so powerful, don't you agree?" Master Lau said. She heard a kind of expectation in his voice. What was it that he wanted her to say? Then she understood: He wanted her to feel the same way. To hunger for power, like he did.

How should she answer? Cassidy studied his face a moment. "I guess it feels good to know that I can take care of myself, or that if somebody else was in trouble, I could help them," she finally said. "So, yeah, I guess it's good to be powerful if you use it in the right way."

A shadow crossed her teacher's face, and Cassidy recognized the cloud for what it was. *Master Lau is testing me! That's what this training is all about! He wants me to develop his same sick need for power. If he can't take the coins from me, then he wants me to be as evil as he is—he wants me on his side!*

❀ Chapter Nine

Saturday afternoon Cassidy took the ferry to Bainbridge Island. James had called that morning and suggested she come over. "I found out something about the trip that you need to know," he had said.

On the ferry ride over, Cassidy tried to put her finger on what troubled her about James's phone call. His tone had been casual, but Cassidy thought maybe he was too casual. Something just didn't sound right.

James stood waiting for her at the dock. As she walked down the ramp toward him her heart beat faster. A light breeze ruffled his hair, and he casually flicked it back. *He has no idea how drop-dead gorgeous he is*, she thought.

"Hey," he greeted her. "I'm glad you could come. We really need to talk." His tone was serious, and Cassidy noticed a darkness in his eyes. *He's really worried. What did he find out about the trip?*

On the way to James's house, Cassidy told him about the conversation she'd had with her great-grandmother. When they arrived they went up to his dad's library, lined with shelves of books and glass cases of Chinese antiques and artifacts. James shut the door. "Dad's around somewhere," he explained. "I don't want him to hear any of this, or none of us will be going to Hong Kong."

"What is it, James? You sound—" Cassidy began, but he interrupted her.

"I think I've found out why we're going to Hong Kong in August," he said. "And it has nothing to do with the Wing Chun tournament."

"What?" Cassidy stared at him.

James reached into his pocket and pulled out one of the papers that Master Lau had given them at the end of class on Wednesday. He pointed to the description of the Hungry Ghost Festival that Luis had read.

"Right, I read this. It's a street festival," Cassidy said, not sure why James seemed to be so upset about it. "It's like Halloween or something, right? Lots of food and candy, people in masks, a big bonfire."

"It's been turned into a street festival, but it's way more than that," James said. "It's a very old tradition; it goes back, I don't know, centuries. Maybe longer."

"Okay . . ." Cassidy said, still uncertain of what the problem was.

"It's a time to remember and honor your ancestors. But it's also the night when the gates of the underworld are opened, releasing the hungry ghosts to wander the earth."

"The underworld?" Cassidy repeated. She shook her head and grinned. "You sound like you really believe that stuff. I mean, come on, it's not like ghosts really come out that night or anything, right? It's just a festival—like Halloween. Just for fun."

"Cassidy, come on," James said. "By now you must realize that all this stuff is real. Just like winged snakes and fox demons."

"You're totally right. I guess I'm just beginning to absorb all this," Cassidy said.

"It *is* a night when they come out," James continued. "They're called hungry ghosts because they're looking for anything to devour. But what they're really looking for are *souls* to fill them up." James went over to a stack of books on one end of the table and opened a thick volume to a page he had marked earlier. He began to read: "The hungry ghosts are the spirits who have no one to honor their memory. They are angry and bitter and full of vengeance. Their only relief is the one night of the year when they can satisfy their hunger with the souls of those who have been loved and honored in this world."

Cassidy shivered at the thought of such miserable, tormented creatures. Then she remembered the coin.

"The fifth coin has a ring of faces with their mouths open like they're moaning or screaming," she said, her dread deepening. "Do you think the last coin has something to do with the hungry ghosts?"

"Yeah, I do," James said quietly. "What your great-grandmother warned you about makes sense. She said that unless you saved them, the spirits of your ancestors would all be devoured."

Cassidy could still hear the sharp edge of worry in her great-grandmother's melodic voice. "Yeah, she said that if their spirits were devoured, then I would no longer exist, either." Cassidy recalled the sick sense of foreboding she had felt when she first heard the alarming words.

"Think about it, Cass," James said. "Our trip to Hong Kong just happens to coincide with the one night the hungry ghosts are loose. And what are they looking for? *Souls* to devour!"

Cassidy sat down in a chair at the table and rested her head in her hands, willing herself to calm down so that she could think.

"I'm not sure what we should do, Cass, but we may be in too deep with this," James said carefully. Cassidy sensed that he was holding back just how concerned he really was. "These ghosts are looking for revenge. They're evil and they'll do anything!"

Cassidy wasn't sure she even trusted herself to speak, but she had to know more. She had so many questions! "What do you think Master Lau has to do with this?" she asked James at last. "What does he plan to do? And what does he hope to gain?"

"We know what he wants, right?" James stated. "The coins. He tried to steal them, but the coins have some kind of magic protection. They can't be *taken*, only given. He tried to talk you into giving them to him, but that didn't work, either."

"Right," Cassidy said. "And he can't kill me, because that would still be like taking them." She shook her head. "I still don't get it. I don't know what you're saying."

James seemed to be searching Cassidy's face for something. *He doesn't want to say it*, Cassidy suddenly realized. *He knows something about this that he wants me to figure out on my own.*

Cassidy thought over her great-grandmother's words again. *Unless you save us, our spirits will be devoured.... And if we cease to exist, then there can be no YOU!*

"Oh my God—that's how he can take the

coins!" Cassidy suddenly felt as if all the air had been sucked out of the room and the walls were closing in on her. "If he can get the hungry ghosts to devour my ancestors' spirits, then I'll cease to exist! And then he can take the coins because it will be like I never had them!"

James didn't have to say a word. The look on his face told Cassidy that he had already come to the same terrifying conclusion.

Chapter Ten

Cassidy had been tossing in her bed for hours. Her clock clicked over to two A.M., and she thought about going downstairs for something to drink. Her cat, Monty, lay in a ginger-colored curl at the end of the bed, undisturbed by Cassidy's restless night.

Thoughts thrashed inside Cassidy's head, darting from one dark realization to another. *Master Lau plans to do something so that the hungry ghosts will devour the spirits of my ancestors.* She and James had wondered how he planned to make it happen and guessed that the ritual Cassidy had witnessed him performing in his office had something to do with it. "Maybe," James had suggested, "he was practicing."

Cassidy sat up in bed and reached out to touch the shrine next to her bed. *My ancestors! I have to do something. It's all up to me.*

But she didn't think she was ready for something like this. Maybe James was right—they were in too deep. Maybe she shouldn't even go to Hong Kong.

But as soon as she had the thought, she realized that this was not an option. *Whether I'm there or not, Lau plans to do something. My ancestors have said that it's up to me. I can't let them down. Somehow my destiny is tied up with this trip to Hong Kong.*

She remembered how powerful she had felt during her last training session with Master Lau. *I could have taken him down*, she realized. *I have a chance— maybe a good chance—at defeating him. I have to try.*

A faint orange glow appeared next to Cassidy's bed. At first she thought she was seeing the rising sun, but then she realized it was far too early. The orange glow formed into two columns, and then Cassidy's ancestors Ng Mui and Wing Chun appeared, radiant in tangerine and apricot silk. Their presence brought an instant warming comfort to Cassidy.

"*Daughter of Light,*" Ng Mui said, "*time is a wave, and tonight we will ride this wave back through the years.*"

"*Come with us, Mingmei,*" Wing Chun said, and reached her hand out to Cassidy.

Before Cassidy even knew what was happening, she was lifted up. She looked down and saw herself asleep in bed — one arm thrown over her head. Monty woke up and looked toward the ceiling, his whiskers twitching.

I'm suspended or floating or something! Cassidy realized with a start. *How is this possible?* Ng Mui and Wing Chun were on either side of her, and each woman held their hands out to her. She placed her hands in theirs and felt their warmth course through her, but also realized that she couldn't feel the firmness of flesh and bone.

In the next moment, she and the two women had flown out the window and into the dark night. The worries seemed to drain from her mind as she flew faster and faster through space. Down below, she saw dark patches of colors, purple, blue, and black, and she wondered how high she was flying. Ahead she saw tiny pinpoints of starlight that blurred as she flew past them.

She wanted to say something, to ask the two women where they were going, but she couldn't form any words. It was as if her lungs were emptied of air and filled with something much lighter — something that lifted her out of her earthbound body and allowed her to fly. She had never felt so free, and wished the journey could last forever.

Suddenly Cassidy noticed that they were slowing down. She could make out large rectangles of greens and browns down below. *Fields,* she thought. Dotted across the landscape here and there were small villages.

Cassidy and the women flew closer and closer to earth, and then stopped. They seemed to be suspended in midair above a small, dusty courtyard. Two boys sat together on a low stone bench beneath the lacy leaves of a pale green tree.

My grandfather! Cassidy realized immediately. Even as a teen, the white, feathery streak against his shiny dark hair was a giveaway. *But who's the other guy?*

Ng Mui leaned in toward Cassidy. *"Listen closely,"* she said, *"and your question will be answered, my daughter."* Cassidy heard the words of the two boys drift up through the heart-shaped leaves of the tree.

Cassidy's grandfather lifted the top of a wooden box. *It's the box of coins!* Cassidy recognized the intricate wood carvings on the small box immediately.

"This is my birthday gift," her grandfather said. "From my father. But they're not to spend; they're to keep. He said that I will know what to do with them when the time is right."

Her grandfather reached into the box and took out the coins. Cassidy could tell by the way he held them that they felt heavy in his hand.

"Can I see them?" the other boy asked. "I want to hold them."

"Just for a moment," said Cassidy's grandfather. He placed the five coins in the eager and open hands of his friend.

The boy held the coins and closed his fingers over them. He shut his eyes for a moment. Cassidy noticed that her grandfather frowned, obviously puzzled by his friend's odd behavior.

"Give them back now," her grandfather said.

The boy opened his eyes, and Cassidy saw a darkness there that she hadn't seen before. But it was a darkness that looked familiar.

"These coins are powerful!" the boy said, his voice as dry as the yellow dust that swirled in the courtyard where they sat.

She knew this voice—and those dark, hooded eyes. Master Lau! Her heart quickened as she watched the smooth, unlined face of the boy who would grow up to be her teacher. *He knew my grandfather as a teenager,* Cassidy realized. The questions swirled in her head as she tried to make sense of what she was seeing.

"We can use these coins!" the boy insisted. "I've been studying dark magic, and I can feel the power in these coins. If we can learn how to use their power, we can do anything we want and have anything we want! Just imagine!"

The young boy who was Cassidy's grandfather shook his head and looked at his friend in horror. "Absolutely not!" he said. "Listen to yourself, Chiu Chi! Dark magic? Think about what you are saying!" He took the coins from the hands of Chiu Chi Lau and put them back in the box, closing the lid tightly.

"You are such a fool!" Chiu Chi spat the words. The disgust in his voice was thick and vile. "What do you know about the coins, anyway? They were a gift to you, and they're very powerful. Now you propose to simply lock them away?"

"When the time is right, I will know what I am to do with them," her grandfather said. "I will do what is right."

"You will do what is *right?*" Chiu Chi Lau mocked. "I thought we were friends. The *right* thing to do would be to help your friend. My family was once one of the richest and most powerful families in all of China, and we lost it all. Do you have any idea what an embarrassment that is? But with these coins I can rebuild my family name and share all my successes with you. Think about what we could do together!"

"No," Cassidy's grandfather said firmly. "I will never let you have these coins!" He tucked the wooden box of coins under his arm and hurried away from the courtyard without looking back.

From Cassidy's vantage point above the scene,

she could see Chiu Chi Lau watch her grandfather depart. His narrowed eyes filled with a cold, dark hatred. "You are wrong about that, Li Chen," he declared. "The coins will be mine one day!"

Chapter Eleven

Two weeks later, on the last day of school, Eliza strolled over to Cassidy just as she finished emptying her locker. "Okay, here's my idea," Eliza announced. "You and me. We're going to throw a graduation party! Something really great, like a pool party at my building."

"I don't think I can, Eliza," Cassidy told her, shutting her locker for the last time. "I'm really busy. I've got the tournament coming up in August, remember? That's just two months away. I have a lot of training to do."

"Come on, Cass, this was our *last* year at Cleary Street Middle," Eliza said. "You have to help me. It'll be fun!"

Last . . . last . . . last. That was the only word that Cassidy heard lately. More and more she found herself feeling that she was doing many things for the last time. The words *uncertain future* had played a continual loop in her head for the past few weeks.

She slung her backpack over her shoulder. *Don't think like that,* she ordered herself. "All right," she told Eliza as they left the building. "I guess I can help out."

"Wow, that's some enthusiasm," Eliza said dryly. "It's a *party* we're planning—not a funeral." When Cassidy didn't laugh, or even smile, Eliza stopped right in the middle of the sidewalk.

"Okay, what's going on?" Eliza demanded, her hands on her hips. "You've been acting really down for a while. And now you don't even want to do this party with me. Which I hoped might actually cheer you up."

"Nothing's wrong, Eliza," Cassidy said, wishing that Eliza would drop it. "Everything's fine—I'm just . . ." She shrugged, not being able to tell her friend what was really bothering her. "Hey, I said I'd help you with the party, okay?"

"I don't get it," Eliza said, shaking her head. "You should be feeling great, Cassidy. School's out.

You've got this amazing summer trip coming up soon. So what's up with the face all the time?"

Cassidy felt a moment of irritation, as if Eliza were trivializing everything that was going on. But she knew that wasn't fair. Eliza had been put in real danger because of Cassidy and the coins. And so the only way Eliza could carry on with the friendship was by pretending the other part of Cassidy's life didn't exist. As a result, Cassidy had stopped trying to talk to her about the coins and about her destiny entirely.

But she can pretend that if she wants, Cassidy thought. *It's not her destiny playing out, it's mine.*

"Well?" Eliza pressed. "What's bugging you?"

Cassidy sighed. She knew that what Eliza wanted to hear was something *normal*. Something about Majesta flirting with James or a fight Cassidy had with her mom. Or even that Cassidy was nervous about the tournament in Hong Kong.

What Cassidy could not say was that she was worried that she might not even make it to Hong Kong. And if she did, that she might not make it back. That there would be some huge, final battle and that Cassidy would fail—and if she did, she would lose *everything*.

"I'm gonna ask you something, Cass," Eliza said. "And I want you to be honest."

Cassidy looked at Eliza—her best friend since forever—then down at her shoes. She felt an ache in her heart that made her want to cry. *Eliza knows that this is about the coins and my destiny, but she doesn't really want to know.*

"I promise I'll be honest, Eliza," Cassidy told her at last. "But be careful what you ask. Don't ask me something that you don't want to hear."

"Then I guess that answers my question," Eliza said. Her normally bright blue eyes darkened, and she took a deep breath.

"So, I'm right, then," Eliza said, and the air seemed to rush out of her. "You've been acting different because of those awful coins. Something is gonna happen and you know it, right?"

Cassidy didn't speak. She just nodded slightly and then looked away before the tears came. Eliza grabbed Cassidy in a strong hug that surprised her. Eliza's voice sounded thick as she said, "I wish you weren't going through all this."

Cassidy almost said, "Me too," which would have been an honest answer. But instead, as she held on tight to her best friend on a busy Seattle sidewalk on her last day of eighth grade, she remembered that the last gift from her ancestors had been the calm mind of a warrior. Cassidy went to that place in her mind that gave her calm strength and gave Eliza the only answer she could: "I have to."

On the way home Cassidy decided that maybe this party would be a good thing after all. Something fun to focus on. She marveled at the way spring was announcing itself in Seattle. Trees held tender green buds that had begun to uncurl into leaves. The sound of the birds seemed more intense, more *insistent*, as if they couldn't contain themselves. Brown lawns were turning pale green as new grass pushed out of what had been the frozen ground of winter. The sea smell even seemed different—rich and abundant with life.

Cassidy suddenly found herself ready to cry. Her throat was hot and tight from trying to hold back the emotion. She thought of Madame Zona's prediction—*your future is uncertain*—and felt as if she were seeing all this beauty for the last time.

So how do I make sure that I have *a future?* she wondered in frustration and fear. The image of the fifth coin rose in her mind, and James's warnings about the festival in Hong Kong. She shuddered. *How can I possibly fight a horde of hungry ghosts?*

Chapter Twelve

Cassidy gazed at the throng of kids surrounding the pool at Eliza's party the following Saturday night. She smiled with satisfaction. She had decided to help Eliza with the party after all, and the two of them had spent the week stringing little white lights in all of the trees. The effect was more than worth it.

"Hey, Wallflower," Luis said, walking up to Cassidy as she admired the banner proclaiming, *We did it!*, which swung from a thick tree branch.

"Very funny, Luis," Cassidy said. "But I'm not a wallflower. I'm an *observer*. There's a difference."

"Yeah, right," Luis said. "No kidding, though, you have a date?"

Cassidy shrugged. "Nah, I'm just here to have fun with my friends."

The words sounded hollow to Cassidy's ears. She certainly didn't feel like having fun. In fact, it felt ridiculous to be standing there at a pool party talking to Luis about having fun when she knew that soon she would have to fight for her very existence!

"Brooke wouldn't come with me," Luis said. Cassidy could hear the disappointment in his voice. "I think she thought that a *middle* school graduation party was too lame." He shrugged. "I guess I'd feel the same way if I were already in high school."

Cassidy looked at Luis. Brooke's rejection was apparent on his face despite the fact that he was trying to cover it up. She knew how he felt. When she had mentioned the party to James, he said he already had plans with Majesta. Again.

"You don't need Brooke," Cassidy told him. "We'll have a good time anyway, okay? We'll hang out, forget about everybody and *everything* else, and have fun."

Luis smiled at her. "Sounds good to me," he said. "You want anything to drink?" he asked her. "Eliza's mom makes killer punch."

"Sure," Cassidy said.

"And after that we'll dance!"

As soon as Luis walked away, Cassidy saw a swirling shadow detach itself from his feet. Her insides went cold as she realized what she was seeing. Just inches away from her, three shadowy dark ghosts were whirling and twisting about. She took a step and noticed that they moved with her. Smoky dark and mostly unformed, each of the transparent phantoms had a hideous, tortured-looking face with dark, bottomless eye sockets and a rounded mouth, opened in what looked like a permanent moan—just like the permanent moan on the faces of the fifth coin.

One of the phantoms looked up at her, and its mouth opened and closed. Cassidy gasped.

It's trying to tell me something!

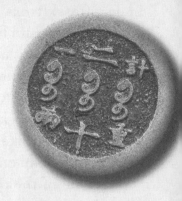

❧ Chapter Thirteen

What's happening? Terrified, Cassidy wondered if this was it. Was this the beginning of the showdown with the demons her ancestors warned her about— the demons of the fifth coin?

Was she going to have to fight these . . . *things,* whatever they were, right here at Eliza's party? *No!* screamed the voice inside Cassidy's head as she looked around at everyone. *There are too many people here! My friends!* Cassidy would never forgive herself if anyone got hurt because of her.

"Hey, Cassidy!" Eliza bounded up to her. "We did great! Totally rocking party, if I do say so myself."

Cassidy couldn't respond. She noticed that one of the ghostly figures whirled closer around her. She took a step back, and again the dark mass moved with her. *It's like they're attached to me!* she realized with growing horror.

"Earth to Cassidy?" Eliza teased.

Cassidy stared at Eliza. It was almost incomprehensible to her that Eliza couldn't see what was going on. The murky spirits were all over both of them now. One grotesque face loomed over Eliza's shoulder and peered at Cassidy with empty, mournful eyes. She quickly put her hand to her mouth, afraid she might be sick.

"You okay?" Eliza asked her, concern crossing her face. "You look kind of weird."

"I . . . I need to go home," Cassidy stammered. She had to get out of there. She had to keep the dark ghosts away from Eliza and anybody else who might come near her.

"Are you sure?" Eliza said, sounding disappointed. "Maybe if you —"

"Eliza," Cassidy said firmly, cutting her off. "I have to go."

Eliza's blue eyes widened. "Is there something freaky going on here? Cassidy, don't tell me —"

"Everything will be okay," Cassidy promised, "as long as I get out of here right now."

Cassidy darted through the crowd and left the pool area, scurrying around to the front of the apartment building. She sensed without even having to look that the spirits were still with her. She stopped on the sidewalk in front of the building and shook her arm hard. The ghostly figure that clung to it was shaken loose for a moment, but immediately returned and clutched her arm once again. The yellow glow of a nearby streetlamp cast eerie shadows and illuminated the inky spirits that continued to encircle her, pulling at her, tugging, almost as if they were pleading with her.

"What do you want?" she asked, all her senses alert and focused, ready to fight if necessary. "Why are you doing this?"

One smoky gray spirit seemed to detach itself from the other two and positioned itself to face Cassidy. She could just make out a high-pitched hum that began deep in the dark thing's throat. *What is it trying to tell me?* The hairs along her neck prickled as a piercing tone shattered the quiet night.

Cassidy felt paralyzed, fixed to the ground by the spirits that covered her in their dark cocoon of misery. The ghosts' hum escalated to a shriek as it moved closer to her face. Cassidy squeezed her eyes shut and clapped her hands over her ears.

Breathe! Slow, calm, steady—just breathe! "Help me," she cried out to her ancestors. "Please help me!"

The earsplitting shriek ended on a thin, sorrowful note that hung in the air for a moment and then disappeared. Was it all over? Cassidy opened her eyes and gasped. She saw that she now stood under a misty dome of silvery light. The hideous specters were gone, and she felt free of their gloomy heaviness.

The light around her began to dissipate and then rise before vanishing entirely into the starry night sky above her. "Thank you," Cassidy whispered, her voice shaking with emotion. She knew it was her ancestors who had responded to her cries for help.

Cassidy walked the few blocks home, keeping a nervous eye out for any movement in the shadows between houses and in the dense foliage of the evergreens that lined the street. The cry of a neighborhood cat made her jump and clutch her throat.

She tried to block out the horrifying image of the ghosts' repulsive, openmouthed faces. *Just like the spirits that Master Lau had called out of the flames.*

As she reached her house she saw the warm, welcoming light that bathed the front lawn in a pale glow. Through one of the windows, she noticed her dad in his office, head bent over some papers on his desk, probably working on the family chart.

Cassidy fought the urge to run into the house, to tell her parents everything, to beg them to do something, *anything*, to stop the inevitable from happening.

 Chapter Fourteen

"Are you all right?" Eliza asked the minute Cassidy answered the phone the next morning. "What happened?"

"Nothing. I just needed to go, okay?" Cassidy wished Eliza wouldn't press this. She knew Eliza would be horrified hearing about the dark spirits at her party.

There was a long silence. "Tell me, Cassidy. I already know it had something to do with those stupid coins."

Cassidy squeezed her eyes shut, willing herself

not to cry. "Yes," she said. "I'm so sorry. I left so that it wouldn't spoil your party."

"Did they hurt you?" Eliza asked. Cassidy could hear the concern, her genuine worry.

"I'm all right. And they didn't do anything to anyone else, either, but I was afraid that they might. That's why I left . . ."

"So it's over now," Eliza said decisively.

"No," Cassidy admitted in a small voice. "Not . . . not yet."

Eliza sighed. "I guess you really have to see this destiny thing through," she said, "or this is just going to keep happening."

"Right," Cassidy said, a surge of gratitude rising in her. Finally Eliza understood. It was really great to know that even if she still didn't want to talk about it, Eliza *got* it.

"Somehow this all ties into your trip to Hong Kong," Eliza said.

"Yes."

"I wish I could help you," Eliza said.

"I know," Cassidy said. "But don't worry, I have someone who can." She said goodbye to Eliza, then called James to set up a time and place to meet.

❧❧❧❧❧

"Those were definitely hungry ghosts that you saw, Cassidy," James said once they found seats at the Ethos Café. It felt good to know that she and James were finally becoming comfortable around each other again. She still burned in embarrassment every time she thought about the awful things her darker half said to James, but he never brought it up and neither did she.

"But I thought they came out during that festival in August," Cassidy said.

"You know what I think?" James said. "I bet whatever Master Lau was doing in his office that day allowed him to open the gates to the underworld early."

The café was almost empty, but James was careful to keep his voice low. "I found another book about the Hungry Ghost Festival. Kind of the history and the different traditions. I read that people who lived near rivers or the sea would float lanterns in the water to keep the bad spirits away from their homes and villages. I think there's something about the light . . ."

"Yeah, when I called on my ancestors for help," Cassidy told James, "it was like I was in this bubble of light. Like it was protecting me or something."

"I guess it was kind of dark at the party, right?" James asked. "And that's where you saw them?"

"Yeah, they were *clinging* to me."

"I don't know if this helps, Cass," James said, "but I don't think they have a lot of power yet. To do evil things, I mean."

"Like devour the souls of my ancestors?" Cassidy asked, the words sounding unbelievable to her ears.

"Yeah, I don't think they can really do much harm until the night of the Hungry Ghost Festival, when they're all released."

Cassidy recoiled at the thought of more cursed spirits like the three who had attached themselves to her at Eliza's party. "What am I supposed to do, James?" she asked. The fear felt like a solid object at the back of her throat. "I'm sure it was my ancestors who protected me last night, but they can't help me if these creatures are able to devour their souls. I'll be all alone!"

James was quiet for a moment, and it seemed to Cassidy that he might be looking into some dark place in the future. He reached over and lightly squeezed her shoulder. "I'll be there with you, Cassidy. I'll help you any way I can."

Cassidy's skin tingled where James had touched her. In spite of everything, she felt happy at this moment. *If only everything could be normal so that James and I could be . . .*

But she wasn't sure how to finish the sentence. Cassidy knew that James was probably not interested in her as anything but a friend. It was as a friend he had offered her his help, his promise to be there with her.

Ever since the night that James happened upon Cassidy in the woods fighting the winged snake demon, she had told him everything. Everything except one very small piece of the puzzle that she'd left out.

"James, remember when I told you about that first dream? The one I had the night of my fourteenth birthday?" Cassidy said.

"Yeah, that's when your ancestors told you about your destiny, right?" James said.

"Yeah, well, I learned one other thing that night that I've never mentioned," Cassidy said. "I don't know why I didn't tell you. Maybe it was because I wanted to be sure."

"What was it, Cassidy?" James said. "Just tell me."

Cassidy took a deep breath. How would he react to what she had to say? It might not be something he'd want to hear. *Or he could tell me I'm crazy.*

But Cassidy knew that it was too late to back up. She'd already said too much for him to let it go. Besides, if she was right, this was something that he needed to know. "Just before leaving, one of the women said, 'Being a warrior is a lonely fate. But an ally will find you. Be careful of whom you trust.'"

James was silent for a moment. He looked down at the table as if he might be studying the pattern in the wood grain. Cassidy's stomach churned. What was he thinking? *Is he sorry that he ever got mixed up in all this?*

"So you think I'm that ally?" James asked her quietly. He brought his eyes to meet hers.

Cassidy looked at him, trying to read his expression. "You showed up about a week later in Wing Chun. And you've been there to help me ever since."

"Wait, let me get this straight," James said. "You think I might actually be part of this whole *destiny* thing?"

Cassidy didn't answer. She wasn't sure there was anything left to say.

James gazed out the window, where the Seattle sun burned like an orange flame in the western sky. "Okay," he said tentatively. "I guess . . . I guess I'm cool with that . . . I think."

They sat in silence for a moment, the lonely cry of a gull the only sound to break the stillness. The creaky wooden door to the café opened, and Cassidy and James looked up to see Master Lau cross to the counter. He noticed the two of them at the back table, frowned slightly, and then gave a slight nod of acknowledgment before placing his order.

After he left the café and the door closed behind him, James leaned in close to Cassidy. "The woman told you to be careful about who you trust, right?" he said. "One guess who she was talking about."

 Chapter Fifteen

As the plane taxied down the runway at the Sea-Tac Airport on a bright August morning Cassidy felt her stomach in her throat. The engines were at full throttle as the jet lifted up into the perfect blue Seattle sky. Cassidy peered out the window as they left the city skyline behind and headed out over the Pacific.

"Bye, Mom, I love you," Cassidy whispered, her breath fogging the tiny window. She had spent all of July preparing for what had been feeling more and more like the final battle. She had worked for long hours training alone in her favorite secluded spot, an abandoned playground full of dilapidated equipment.

She had honed her skills so that she could deliver deadly blows and surprise kicks that would take down someone more than twice her size. *But will it be enough?* she had asked herself over and over. *Can I save my ancestors—and myself?*

"Nervous, honey?" her dad asked, placing his hand over hers on the armrest between them. She saw that her knuckles were white from gripping the seat. Cassidy smiled at her father.

"I guess so," she told him. He had no idea, of course, what she was actually referring to.

"Why don't you push your seat back and take a nap? It's going to be a long flight."

"It's okay, Dad," Cassidy told him. "Maybe later."

But despite her intention to stay awake, the drone of the engine and the early hour they had gotten up made her sleepy. She dreamed that she was hurtling through darkness toward some unknown horror, and she woke with a start.

"Whoa, there," Luis said. "You almost jumped out of your seat."

Cassidy rubbed her eyes and tried to remember where she was. A plane, on her way to Hong Kong for the Wing Chun tournament and who knew what else. "Where's Dad?" she asked.

"Switched seats," Luis answered as he turned his attention back to the Game Boy in his hands. "He wanted to talk to Master Lau. Were you dreaming just now, or what?"

Cassidy remembered the terrifying feeling of falling through dark and empty nothingness. "Yeah, nightmare."

"You missed lunch or dinner or whatever you call the stuff they brought through earlier. The time of day is all mixed up. It was really early when we left, and now it's like so much later. So weird. I bet we'll be jet-lagged out of our minds."

Cassidy looked out the window. She could see the silver wing of the plane just ahead of her as it cut through the rapidly darkening sky. Wisps of gray clouds hung in the air below them like sooty clumps of cotton.

"I think I need to stretch my legs," Cassidy said. She pushed herself up, and Luis turned sideways so that Cassidy could step out into the narrow aisle. She walked toward the restrooms at the back of the plane. Majesta and James sat several seats behind Cassidy's row. James was flipping through a magazine, and Majesta had fallen asleep, her head resting lightly on his shoulder. Jealousy started to take hold of Cassidy, as it did every time she saw James and Majesta together. But she stopped the negative thought before it could go further. One lesson that Cassidy had learned was that controlling her emotions and defeating her dark side was a daily battle that had to be fought.

James glanced up and saw Cassidy. "Hanging in there?" he asked quietly.

Cassidy shrugged. "I guess. I fell asleep. Weird, scary dreams."

There was a sudden jolt and the plane lurched. Cassidy pitched forward and almost landed in James's lap.

Majesta's head jerked up. "What?" she mumbled, confused. The seat belt warning signs came on, and a flight attendant made the announcement that everyone should return to their seats.

As Cassidy made her way back the plane felt like a bucking bronco, the floor dropping and then coming back up again.

Luis had already fastened his seat belt, and Cassidy stepped across him to get into her seat.

"This is Captain Hobson. We are experiencing some turbulence and would like to ask everyone to remain in their seats with their seat belts on. If you need assistance, please ring for an attendant."

"Is it just me, or did the captain sound kind of tense?" Luis asked Cassidy. "What is turbulence exactly, anyway?"

"I don't know. I guess it's like wind or whatever that the plane has to fly against." Cassidy peered out the window into a night that was purplish black. The lights from the plane illuminated the wisps of clouds surrounding the wing.

Cassidy pressed her face closer to the window and frowned. Something wasn't right. The grayish clouds swirled around the wing, and then one cloud seemed to detach from the rest and fly up against the window where Cassidy sat staring. Suddenly the cloud changed shape. Before Cassidy realized what was happening, a grotesque and evil face pressed against the glass.

The ghosts! The hungry ghosts! Fear gripped her heart as the plane lurched violently. She stared in horror as the ghosts began pushing up and down on the wing of the plane, causing it to tip from side to side!

In the next second all went black as the interior lights of the plane blinked out. Several heavy thuds told Cassidy that some of the luggage was falling out of the overhead bins. A passenger screamed, and there were muffled cries of concern as the flight attendants tried to restore order in almost total darkness.

"What's happening?" Luis asked. Cassidy could tell by his voice that he was totally freaked out.

"It's gonna be okay, Luis," she said, holding tightly to the armrest. "Probably just some kind of electrical problem."

The lights flickered once and then went off again as the plane continued to lurch, rolling from one side to another and back again. And then for a brief moment, the plane seemed to pull out of whatever turbulence it had just experienced. Cassidy could feel and hear the power of the engines as they strained to move the huge jet forward through the night.

She looked out the window again, straining to see if the ghosts were still attacking the plane. A small exterior light showed that they were still there — but there was something else out there, too. Something in the distance heading toward them. Cassidy caught her breath as she realized that the dark cloud moving swiftly toward the plane was an entire swarm of hungry ghosts.

When they arrived, they covered the entire surface of the plane and began pushing against it. The plane tilted violently to the left and then back to the right. The engines strained as the captain struggled to regain control of the jet and keep it on its steady path. The captain's announcement crackled over the speakers. In a voice edged with tension, he asked everyone to remain calm and explained that they would pass through the area of turbulence shortly.

Cassidy looked at Luis in the seat beside her. In the dim glow of the emergency lights, she could see that his face was pale. Luis was trying to hold it together, but Cassidy could read the fear in his eyes.

"It's gonna be okay . . ." she started to say. But before the words were out of her mouth, the plane tipped forward and began a rapid and sickening descent toward earth.

🌸 Chapter Sixteen

Screams ripped through the darkness inside the plane, louder than the groan of the jet engines. Cassidy felt herself pushed forward so hard and fast that the seat belt cut into her stomach. Her head bumped against the back of the seat in front of her. *No!* her mind screamed.

Then there was a change, subtle at first but gradually more noticeable. Cassidy had the sensation of being lifted, of rising. The plane began to right itself. Cassidy was now upright and leaning back in her seat again. *What's going on? Did the ghosts leave?* Had the pilot gained control?

She looked out the window into the dark night sky and saw that an eerie glow encircled them. A ring of silvery light like an incandescent mist enveloped the plane.

The captain made several announcements to reassure the passengers that they had passed safely through the turbulence and that he expected a smooth flight the rest of the way to Hong Kong. The flight attendants were kept busy taking care of frightened passengers and putting away luggage and other items that had fallen out of the overhead storage.

The light. Was it my ancestors? Cassidy wasn't sure, but whatever it was, it protected the plane all the way to the airport in Hong Kong.

෬෬෬෬෬

Cassidy's dad looked ashen as they exited the plane together. He kept his arm tightly around Cassidy and told her over and over that he was sorry he had switched seats with Luis. "It's okay, Dad," she had assured him. "We're all fine now."

As they walked down the ramp into the crowd waiting at the gate James caught up to her. While her father talked to the customs officer James tugged her arm, pulling her away from her dad.

"Okay, was that just a really bad flight, or was

it, you know, something else?" he whispered.

She looked at him and nodded. "It was . . . something else."

He ran his hand nervously through his dark hair. "I kinda thought so," he said. "I didn't think we were gonna make it there for a minute."

"Me either," she said. "I don't know if I can do this, James." Her voice was choked with both relief at being on solid ground once again and the paralyzing terror of what lay ahead.

"Do you have a choice?" James asked.

"No." She thought that she had never felt as tired as she did at that moment. "I have to do the right thing, James," she said.

Up ahead of them, Cassidy watched Master Lau motioning the Wing Chun team over to a van that waited at the curb. "I have to fight whatever comes next," she said. "My life and the life of my family depends on it."

The weight of what lay ahead of Cassidy rested heavily on her shoulders as the van sped away from the busy airport and headed toward the hotel. Cassidy heard the excited voices of the other students as they looked out the windows at the exotic scenery all around.

I wish I could enjoy this, Cassidy thought. *I wish I could just be a normal girl on this amazing trip with my friends.*

Near the water on the left side, Cassidy saw a man and two children walking toward a fishing pier. The man held several cane poles in one hand and a wicker basket in the other. The two young children followed closely behind their father, talking to each other excitedly.

As the van rumbled past the pier and turned a corner Cassidy saw hundreds of colorful banners draped across the entrance to a floating restaurant. A long wooden walkway led from the sidewalk across the water to the sprawling restaurant that floated at the edge of the water.

"Specials! Best specials in all of Hong Kong! Come get your discounts!" a young man shouted from the sidewalk. He handed out neon pink discount coupons to every pedestrian who walked past him.

"Discounts are good for one week!" the man shouted to the throngs of tourists.

I wonder if I'll still be around in a week, Cassidy thought gloomily.

ⓐⓐⓐⓐⓐ

The Victoria Harbor Hotel was a tall, modern, glass-and-steel structure overlooking the busy harbor. As the group hustled inside, Cassidy caught a glimpse of large ferryboats and small fishing boats on the water.

In the plush red-and-gold-accented hotel lobby Cassidy and the others waited while Master Lau and the chaperones checked in at the desk and picked up their keys. Luis had gotten over his earlier terror and was keyed up about the team practices they would do later in the day. Majesta was chatting with one of the girls that she knew from another Wing Chun studio in Seattle. Cassidy glanced through the tourist brochures in a rack near the front desk.

Cassidy's dad was talking on the phone at a nearby kiosk. He caught her eye and winked. He was smiling broadly and motioned for her to come over. As he hung up the phone he explained that he had been speaking to his cousin that he hadn't seen in over twenty years.

"We were just boys when I saw him last. He's on his way in. In fact, he was just parking his car when I reached him on his cell phone."

"That's great, Dad," Cassidy said. "So you two are going to catch up?"

"Yes, he's going to take me to see his elderly mother, my aunt. She's in poor health." He looked over at a flower wagon parked just outside the large open doors of the hotel. "I'll buy some flowers for her. What about you, Cass? Do you want to go with us, or do you and the team have other plans?"

"Well, I'd love to meet all my cousins, but we have a practice scheduled for this afternoon."

"Yes, that's right. I forgot," Simon replied. "There'll be time later. Your mother warned me about taking up all your time in Hong Kong with visits to my family."

"No, really, I want to meet them," Cassidy said.

"Simon Chen?" a man said, approaching Cassidy and her father. "Cousin Simon Chen?"

Cassidy's dad turned and found himself wrapped in the warm embrace of his cousin. "Stephen!" Simon cried. "Look at you—you're an old man now!"

Stephen Chen laughed and said, "I guess that means you're old, too! We're the same age and you know it! We've even celebrated birthdays together in the past."

Simon laughed and turned to Cassidy. "Stephen, this is my daughter, Cassidy. I expect she'll be leaving Hong Kong with several trophies at the end of this trip."

Stephen greeted Cassidy warmly. "Your father's told me all about your Wing Chun skills," he said. "You must be quite honored to represent Master Chiu Chi Lau's team here in Hong Kong."

"Do you know Master Lau?" Cassidy asked, startled that her cousin knew Master Lau's full name.

"He built quite a reputation as a *shifu* here in Hong Kong," Stephen said. "Very strict teacher, very disciplined. Did you know that he was once friends with our family?"

"He was?" Simon asked. "When was that?"

"Actually, your father and Chiu Chi Lau were boyhood friends. They grew up in the same village just outside the city."

"That's very odd," Simon said, and his forehead creased. "I just spent several hours on the plane next to him and he never mentioned it."

"It's very likely that he doesn't know you're the son of Li Chen," Stephen told him. "The only reason I know is that my mother remembers the two boys playing together. Then there was some kind of argument, I think, and the boys drifted apart."

Cassidy remembered her journey back through time with her two ancestors. She couldn't help thinking about what the teenage Lau had said to her grandfather that night. "The coins will be mine one day," he had vowed. Cassidy could not shake the unsettling feeling of dread that that day could come very soon.

✿ *Chapter Seventeen*

Cassidy was not thrilled to be sharing a room with Majesta Madison, but there was nothing she could do about it. She was certain that Majesta wasn't any happier about the arrangement than she was.

"I wish we didn't have a practice scheduled this afternoon," Majesta said as she unpacked her suitcase and set out an astonishing array of cosmetics on the dresser.

"Yeah, me too," Cassidy admitted. The flight had been terrifying and exhausting. What she wanted to do was take a very long nap, but they had been told that staying up and active the first day would be the best way to adapt to the time difference and get past their jet lag. Cassidy figured that was the reason a practice had been planned for the afternoon.

Cassidy removed her workout sweats from her bag and put them in a small backpack to take along with her. Then she took out her outfit for the tournament and placed it on a hanger. Master Lau had asked his students to order a custom silk wushu uniform to use during competition. Cassidy's uniform was a deep midnight blue, so dark that it almost looked black. Cassidy remembered that Master Lau had been very specific about which colors they could choose from. Luis's uniform was a dark turquoise, Majesta's was a dark green, and James's was a deep purple.

Just as Cassidy was hanging up her uniform, there was a knock at the door. "Master Lau wants us downstairs in five," said Luis.

"Yeah, yeah, we're on our way," Majesta called back, rolling her eyes for Cassidy to see.

❧❧❧❧❧

Master Lau was waiting in the hotel lobby with three other *shifus* from the Seattle area who had accompanied them on the trip. Cassidy noticed that the other teachers were smiling, and even seemed to be joking around with one another and a few students who had already gathered. Master Lau stood apart from the others and glanced several times toward the clock on the far wall.

Cassidy and Majesta joined Luis and James just as one of the *shifus* introduced himself and called everyone to order.

"I'm Shifu Curtis Karder from the Fleet Road Academy, and I hope everyone is as excited and honored to be here in Hong Kong as I am." The four students from Shifu Karder's class gave a small cheer. Cassidy looked at Luis, who had raised his eyebrows. She knew what he was thinking. Shifu Karder had a much more casual approach than Master Lau, who would definitely have frowned on this public display of emotion.

While Shifu Karder outlined for the students what to expect during the next few days, Cassidy observed Master Lau. *Definitely distracted,* she realized. *He's glancing at the door and then back at the clock, like, every couple of minutes.* Cassidy looked at James, and she saw that he was also keeping a close eye on their teacher.

"It's just a short walk over to the Hong Kong Martial Arts Academy," Master Karder said as he began leading the group toward the door. "We'll have a chance to see where the tournament will be held, and I also believe they have a couple of practice rooms reserved for us."

As they followed the group out onto the sidewalk, James walked over to Cassidy. "What's going on with Lau?" he whispered.

Cassidy shrugged. "Seems kind of nervous or . . . maybe anxious."

"Yeah, kind of anxious and excited—but not about the competition. Have you noticed he showed zero interest in anything Shifu Karder told us? I'm telling you, Cass, he's definitely not here for the tournament."

The small group of students and their teachers walked down the busy Hong Kong sidewalk passing stores with windows showcasing jade, porcelain, gold jewelry, silks, carpets, and furniture. Cassidy kept her eye on the back of Master Lau's head. The other teachers looked from side to side, taking in all the sights and sounds of the beautiful city, but Master Lau walked very straight. *What are you thinking right now?* Cassidy wondered. *If you're not thinking about the tournament in two days—a tournament that we've been preparing for during the last six months—then what are you thinking about?*

As they turned the corner, Shifu Karder pointed out a large banner stretched between two posts at the entrance to the academy. WELCOME UNITED STATES KUNG FU ASSOCIATION, the banner read.

"A picture!" Shifu Karder called out, and began pulling a small digital camera from his pocket.

"Everyone under the banner!"

A young woman stepped over and said, "Let me take the photo for you so that you can be in the picture, too."

As the group gathered under the banner, Cassidy noticed that Master Lau was not with them. He stood by himself near a large sign, just out of the photo, looking down the street.

ର/ର/ର/ର/ର

Instead of a gym or studio, the Seattle groups were taken to a flat lawn for their practice session. Cassidy saw several other groups going through sparring drills and wooden dummy practice with their teachers.

Cassidy, Majesta, Luis, and James stood with Master Lau as he directed them to begin with *chi sau*. Cassidy was paired with James. The afternoon Hong Kong sun warmed her face, giving it a golden glow, and she felt that she could stand out there practicing sticking hands with James Tang forever.

While they concentrated on the drills Cassidy allowed herself to forget about the hungry ghosts and Master Lau's plan for a few minutes. As she moved in close, James blocked, then Cassidy feigned to the right and went in for a hold, catching James off guard.

Out of habit she looked toward Master Lau. It

was just the kind of move that would have impressed him. But Master Lau hadn't seen the hold at all. He stood with his back to his four students and gazed out across the blue water in Victoria Harbor. He seemed to be looking toward a distant mountain, covered in green and gold, whose flattened peak reached up into the sky.

Chapter Eighteen

"Thank God we're not competing until tomorrow," Majesta said the next morning as they returned to their room after breakfast. "I think I'm more wiped out today than I was yesterday."

"Yeah, kind of delayed jet lag, I guess," Cassidy said. Majesta began examining her face closely in the large mirror over the dresser. "My skin looks horrible! I've actually got dark circles under my eyes!"

"No, you don't," Cassidy said, which was exactly what she knew Majesta expected her to say. "You look fine."

"Yeah? Okay, yeah, I guess I look pretty good. I mean, considering the trip and then that practice yesterday. I hate getting stuck with Luis for sticking hands. He's so—"

Cassidy finished the sentence for her. "He's so good, Majesta," she said. "Luis has been practicing a lot. He really wants to do well in this tournament."

"Well, so do I," Majesta said. "All of us want to do well. I'm just glad we get a day off for fun. So which one of the activities did you sign up for?" Majesta asked. Cassidy wondered if she was asking just so she could make sure to not do the same thing.

"The museum one," Cassidy said with a shrug. She hoped to use her time in the museum to research the coins. The tournament was not the only event that began tomorrow. The Hungry Ghost Festival did, too. Cassidy had seen a poster in the hotel lobby inviting all the guests to come to the Chinese Lion Dance and afterward, the bonfire of the Hungry Ghost god. *Each year we invite our hotel guests to kick off the Hungry Ghost Festival with us*, the poster read. *Come along and celebrate this traditional festival!*

"Sounds like fun," Luis had said as they read the poster together. "We are so lucky to be here when this festival thing's going on."

Yeah, lucky, Cassidy had thought, feeling her blood run cold. *If Master Lau has anything to do with it, the Hungry Ghost Festival will be anything but lucky for me.*

Cassidy began looking through her duffel bag for the small package that contained her warrior shrine. She hadn't taken it out the day before but decided now that she needed to see it and touch it.

"We're taking the boat trip out in Victoria Harbor," Majesta said. Cassidy noticed the *we* that Majesta had used and was certain that she was including James in her sightseeing plans.

"Yeah, that sounds like fun, too," Cassidy said. "But this museum has some really great things. Ancient stuff that I want to see."

"I don't really like musty old museums. In fact, I don't like any kind of old stuff. I think it's kind of depressing," Majesta declared.

Cassidy found her warrior shrine and removed it from the paper. *How will Majesta feel about this?* Cassidy wondered. *I guess she'll think this is depressing, too.*

Back in Seattle when Cassidy was planning what she would pack, she had almost decided not to include her shrine. But at the last minute she decided that she'd feel better if she had it with her. She remembered the words of the shopkeeper when she bought the beautiful antique. "*It's a warrior's shrine,*" he had said. "*The warrior gathered strength by meditating on the intricate pattern of the leaves.*"

Cassidy ran her fingers over the exquisite carvings and the delicate inlays of gold and jade. "*The jade represented the power necessary to fight,*" the shopkeeper had instructed, "*and the gold reminded the warrior to keep a pure heart even in the midst of battle.*"

A pure heart, Cassidy thought. *I guess that means knowing that you're fighting for the right reason,* she decided.

"What's that?" Majesta asked. She walked over to Cassidy, who had just placed the shrine on the nightstand.

"A warrior shrine," Cassidy explained. "You probably think it's silly that I brought it, but I just like having it with me." Cassidy got ready for some mocking comment.

"No, I don't think it's silly—maybe a little strange—but everybody's got a good luck charm of some kind," Majesta responded, pulling a thin silver chain from around her neck and showing Cassidy the tiny wishbone pendant.

"My mom gave it to me, like, eons ago," Majesta said. "Every time I've worn it in any kind of competition, I've always won! Wing Chun, cheerleading—I even won an essay contest once, and I was wearing it when I wrote the essay."

"I like it," Cassidy said, happy but surprised that Majesta had shared this with her.

"Like I said, we all want to do well in this competition," Majesta said as she tucked the silver pendant back under her T-shirt. "So if your warrior shrine is your good luck charm, I say go for it. Every little bit helps!"

There was a knock at the door, and one of the chaperones called in, "We're meeting in the lobby in ten minutes!"

"I'm going on down," Majesta said. "There's a souvenir shop I want to take a look at."

"I'll be down in a minute," Cassidy said. There was something else she needed to do before going to the museum. After Majesta left the room, Cassidy took the wooden box from her bag and shook the coins out onto the bed. She knew there was a research room at the museum, and she hoped to have some time to find out more about the coins. Then she looked at the clock and saw that she needed to go down to the lobby and meet the others. She quickly dropped the coins into a flat silk pouch that had held her passport. She tied the pouch around her waist, tucking it out of sight under her shirt.

 Chapter Nineteen

Down in the lobby the chaperones stood together in a group and decided who would escort each of the three groups to their sightseeing activities. Cassidy scanned the area but didn't see Master Lau anywhere. *Where could he be? What's he up to? All day yesterday he kept looking at the clock.*

Cassidy spotted James walking toward her. *He looks so good,* she thought as she did every time she saw him. But he didn't seem to be his usual carefree self. There was definitely a shadow in his eyes. *Is it because he's worried about me? Or is he thinking about his mom?*

Does being here make him sad?

Cassidy remembered that at first James hadn't wanted to come on this trip. She had assumed it was because he didn't like Master Lau, but later she learned that Hong Kong was where his mother had died when James was only eight.

James's mother had visited Cassidy as a spirit and had written a message in her foggy mirror about James needing to return to Hong Kong to heal. Cassidy hoped with all her heart that it would happen for him here.

"Hey," James said when he reached Cassidy. "I didn't think you were ever coming down."

"I had to put some stuff away," she told him. "So you and Majesta are going on the boat tour?"

"Majesta is," James said. "I'm not. I'm going to the museum with you. I want to help you with the research while we have time. The first competition starts tomorrow." Cassidy felt like cheering. *James is going with me, not Majesta!* Just as quickly, she realized that there was no reason to gloat. He probably would rather have gone on the boat tour with Majesta, but after what she had told him about being her ally and then what happened on the plane, he probably felt that he had to go with her.

"You sure, James?" Cassidy asked. "I think Majesta is sort of expecting you to go with her."

"It's cool," he said. "I told her that we'd get

together later. Besides, she's got some other friend to go with her."

Cassidy looked across the lobby. Majesta was standing next to a girl from one of the other Seattle classes and the chaperone for the boat tour. She was watching Cassidy and James, but quickly turned when she noticed Cassidy looking her way. Cassidy saw Luis approach the group and remembered that he had signed up for the boat tour, too.

A tall man carrying a clipboard walked up to Cassidy and James. "Looks like we're it," the man said. "I'm Mr. Perkins, the chaperone for the museum tour. James, I understand that you lived here for a number of years."

"Yeah, I was born here," James replied. "My dad and I moved to the States when I was eight."

"You may turn out to be a better guide than I am." Mr. Perkins laughed. "Are you pretty familiar with Hong Kong?"

"I guess so," James said. "My dad taught at the university here. My friends and I hung out in this area all the time."

"It looks like the museum is part of the university," Mr. Perkins said, consulting the brochure attached to his clipboard.

"Yeah, it's a great place, amazing stuff," James said.

"Well, let's go, then," their chaperone said. "I

believe the shuttle is waiting."

On the shuttle ride to the museum, Mr. Perkins chatted with another passenger about a local restaurant he wanted to try. Cassidy and James sat together on the narrow vinyl seat near the back and looked out the open windows as the colorful city blurred past. The skyscrapers towered above them, while down below, the streets bustled with shoppers, tourists, and businesspeople. Vendors called out from every street corner. "Cameras here! Cheap! Best tours, best guides, don't be fooled!" James translated for Cassidy.

As the warm sun bathed her face in a golden light Cassidy felt thrilled to be there—part of the exotic city of Hong Kong—and to be sitting next to James.

The shuttle slowed to a stop while a throng of people crossed the street up ahead. Cassidy noticed an older woman standing on the sidewalk selling oranges from a large fruit cart. With her heightened senses Cassidy smelled the sharp citrus fragrance and wished she had one of the juicy-looking oranges that were stacked pyramid-style on the woman's cart.

Just as the shuttle began moving again, Cassidy saw a dark cloud descend on the cart. At least a dozen shapeless, shadowy figures covered the woman and her fruit cart with their wicked stain of darkness. Cassidy couldn't believe what she was seeing. She wanted to scream to the woman to warn her, but before she could form the words, it was too late.

 Chapter Twenty

In one quick movement the cart was over-turned. Oranges spilled onto the sidewalk and street and rolled under the feet of the pedestrians, who were trying to dodge them. The poor woman tried to grab the handles of the cart and keep it upright, but the handles were wrenched from her hands by the hungry ghosts. Now she sat on the sidewalk looking stunned and angry.

"The ghosts did it," Cassidy told James, her voice low and edged with tension. "I saw them turn over the woman's cart. I wanted to warn her, but I didn't have time!"

James swiveled in his seat and looked back at the chaos. Some people had stopped to help the woman to her feet, while others were setting up her cart again. Several young boys were trying to catch the rolling oranges.

Cassidy watched as the ghosts devoured every orange they could get their hands on, biting into the fruit and letting the sticky juice drip onto the sidewalk. They grabbed the oranges away from each other and shrieked angrily.

"Looks like she's okay," James said. "Are the ghosts still there?"

"Yeah," Cassidy said. "They're stuffing the oranges in their mouths as fast as they can. It's really disgusting."

Cassidy watched with increasing horror as one hungry ghost, its body inky black, its face twisted and mouth open, slithered away from the others and crawled up the side of a building just ahead of them. The creature inched out onto a swinging sign that advertised a shoe repair shop. "Watch," she said to James. She pointed to the sign that had started swinging wildly back and forth.

The grotesque specter yanked the sign from its hooks and let it drop to the sidewalk below. The wood shattered and splintered, barely missing a woman pushing a baby stroller.

"Whoa," James said. "Another ghost?"

Cassidy nodded.

"Lau must be so focused on his plan to get the coins away from you that he's sending some kind of energy your way. I think you're sort of attracting the hungry ghosts because of your connection to Lau."

"You think I'm doing this?" Cassidy hated the idea that she was pulling the horrible creatures toward her—and toward everyone around her.

"No, not you. It's Lau all right," James assured her. "I think he's, like, practicing calling up ghosts. But he doesn't really have control of them yet."

Cassidy wondered if James was right. It made sense—if any of this could make sense. Master Lau had probably already figured out that he couldn't actually kill her and take the coins, so he wasn't sending the ghosts to do her harm. And he would have been just as dead as everyone else if the hungry ghosts had made the plane go down, so it was unlikely he had called them to do that. But then what did he summon them for? If he was practicing how to control hungry ghosts . . . what was he practicing for?

"There are still a lot of holes in this, James," Cassidy said. "Something's not fitting right."

"I know," James admitted as the shuttle pulled up to the glass and wood entrance to the museum. "But maybe the missing puzzle piece is in there."

Mr. Perkins ushered James and Cassidy off the

shuttle and into the cool and open area of the museum lobby. "I understand that there are several different rooms and galleries here," Mr. Perkins said, "each dealing with a different period in China's history. Do you know where you'd like to begin?"

"I know this museum really well, Mr. Perkins," James said. Cassidy was sure she knew where James was going with this. "I wonder if it would be okay if Cassidy and I sort of explored on our own. On the top floor there's a research room and library, and we'd kind of like to hang out up there. If that's okay?"

He's good, very smooth, Cassidy thought. Mr. Perkins frowned. "I suppose that's okay," he said finally. "As long as you don't leave the museum."

James thanked him and assured Mr. Perkins that they wouldn't. They made plans to meet at the front door in two hours.

"That will give us enough time to get back to the hotel and prepare for dinner. I understand that some of the streets will be setting up for the Hungry Ghost Festival, which begins tomorrow," Mr. Perkins said. "Should be interesting to watch."

"Yeah," Cassidy said. "That should definitely be interesting."

James and Cassidy made their way back through a maze of displays toward the bank of elevators at the back of the building. At the door to one room, James stopped and motioned for Cassidy to follow him. "I want to show you something before we go up," he said.

They walked through a dim hallway lined with glass cases lit from the inside. James stopped at one case and motioned for Cassidy to take a look. "See anything familiar?" he asked.

In the long glass case, displayed on a background of rich, gold velvet, was a *nandao*, an antique broadsword. It was an exact replica of the one Cassidy had used to kill the winged snake demon. Seeing it reminded her of how close she was to death that night.

"I guess we better get to work," Cassidy said solemnly.

Her biggest fear was that she didn't know what was going to happen. She didn't know how Master Lau planned to use the hungry ghosts to destroy her. She wondered who she would have to fight—the hungry ghosts or possibly Master Lau himself? Probably both, she figured, and wondered if she could ever be prepared for that battle.

The back of her neck prickled, and she had the strangest sensation that she was being watched. As Cassidy looked up from the case she thought she caught a glimpse of someone slipping around the corner. *A man with dark gray hair, feathered with a white streak!* Cassidy quickly left James's side and ran toward the door that led out into another gallery. She scanned the crowd of people in the room, but didn't see him.

Was that my grandfather? Is he here in Hong Kong? She hurried through the crowded room full of people searching each face, but the person she had seen was gone. Finally she returned to find James standing in the doorway looking for her.

"What happened to you?" he asked.

"I saw a man with dark hair and the white streak like my grandfather's. I thought it might be him," Cassidy explained. "But then he just sort of disappeared."

"You sure it was him?" James asked. "He can't be the only person with dark hair and a gray streak in the front."

Yeah, Cassidy thought as she considered this. "I guess it could have been somebody else."

But as she and James got on the elevator to take them up to the research room Cassidy remembered that she had felt that someone had been watching her. *That's the reason I looked up,* she realized. *He ran when he knew that I'd seen him.*

 Chapter Twenty-One

The research room and library was glassed in on three sides. The magnificent view of Hong Kong and Victoria Harbor took Cassidy's breath away. She looked out over the colorful jumble of concrete and steel buildings, turquoise water, bustling traffic, and thousands of people, and she felt like she was floating above them all. It reminded her of her nighttime flight with her ancestors. She remembered how free she'd felt, and longed for that feeling again—to rise above the sense of doom and fear that she carried with her at all times now.

James sat at a computer terminal searching through a list of books and other materials that were archived in the research room. He printed out a list, and they took it up to one of the assistants. James's father often visited the university in Hong Kong for his work and had been granted research privileges. He had given James a copy of his university ID so that James and Cassidy could have access to the rare and expensive items in the collection.

The woman looked at James's ID and at the list, and asked something in Chinese. James answered, and she smiled. "Then I will speak English," she said with a British accent. She gave them a number and asked them to wait at one of the research tables near the window.

"What do you think we'll find?" Cassidy asked James. "I don't even know what we're looking for."

"I put in a request for several things," James explained. "They actually have the translations of scrolls that were written by some monks about three hundred years ago."

"That was during the time that my two Chinese ancestors Ng Mui and Wing Chun lived," Cassidy said. "Is that why you requested them?"

"Yeah," James said. "The two women probably had the coins made to celebrate their own victories, right? They were both warriors; they told you that in your dream."

"Right," Cassidy agreed, "but what does that have to do with the monks and the scrolls?"

"Some of the monks and even nuns during that time were actually warriors who were trained in secret to defend their temples," James said.

The assistant rolled a cart that held several books and a couple of gray cardboard boxes over to the table where James and Cassidy sat. "Here you are," she said, and then returned to the central desk in the middle of the room.

Cassidy looked at her watch. "Are we going to have time to go through all this?" she asked. "We're meeting Mr. Perkins at four."

"We'll try," James said, lifting one of the cardboard boxes from the stack and opening it, revealing a sheaf of loose papers. "These are copies of the ancient scrolls I told you about. The real scrolls are down in the museum, and they'd never let us actually touch them. Besides, we couldn't read them, anyway. This version includes the translations."

The large, open room was hushed, and there were a few researchers scattered at the tables. Cassidy and James sat close together so they could whisper without disturbing anyone. Her closeness to James made her almost dizzy. There was a clean, soapy smell on his skin, and she was fascinated by his hands as he turned through the pages and pages of translations.

A name on one of the copies caught Cassidy's eye, and she put her hand on James's arm to stop him from turning the page. She pulled the page closer to her so she could read it.

"I think I found something," she said. "This tells about a very powerful warrior monk who was Ng Mui's teacher."

"That's your ancestor!" James said, leaning in to get a closer look. "What else does it say?"

"According to this, Ng Mui showed up at the Shaolin Temple and asked to be accepted as a student. Listen to this. 'She refused to leave, and when another monk challenged her, she defeated him. The Grandmaster allowed her to stay. Within a year she was known as the fiercest warrior in the temple.'"

Cassidy felt the swell of pride within her. *My ancestor—the fiercest warrior in the Shaolin Temple!*

James scanned the next few pages. "Okay, this says that she met Wing Chun, who had been promised in marriage to some guy she didn't love," he said. "According to this, Ng Mui taught Wing Chun how to defend herself against this guy, who said that he would take her as his wife whether she wanted to marry him or not."

Cassidy's eyes pored over the words. "Yeah,

and then the two women became great friends, as close as sisters, and together they developed the fighting animal stances. That's where Wing Chun kung fu came from."

As Cassidy came to the end of the page she leaned back and saw that James was looking at her. "Pretty cool, huh?" he said. "No wonder you're so good, Cass. It's, like, in your genes or something."

Cassidy frowned. "I guess that is pretty cool, but what do we do about the fifth coin and Master Lau? And what about the hungry ghosts?" She tried to keep the panic out of her voice, but she knew her fear was obvious.

James returned the pages to the box and reached for another book. "Let's see if there's anything about the ghosts in here." He flipped open a large black volume to the index, found what he was looking for, and turned to a page near the middle.

Cassidy watched as he read silently. *He's doing this for me,* she thought. *He could be out having fun. He could be with Majesta right now, but he's spending the entire afternoon trying to help me.*

James blinked several times. It looked as if he went back to the top of the page to read the passage over again. "What is it?" she asked him. "Did you find something?"

He swallowed hard before looking up. Cassidy

saw that he was pale. She felt her heart sink. He had found something, and it was bad. "What is it, James? I have to know!"

"He's . . . he's planning a sacrifice! That's how Lau's going to get the ghosts to devour the souls of your ancestors."

An icy chill ran the length of Cassidy's spine as she tried to make sense of what he was saying. "You mean he's going to sacrifice my ancestors?"

"Yes, but there's more to it than that," James said. "Let me read the whole thing to you so I get it right: 'It is believed by some that at the moment of someone's death, the ancestors of the deceased gather to escort the spirit of the newly dead soul. There is a legend that when many spirits are gathered, their energy attracts the hungry ghosts. To die on the night of the Hungry Ghost Feast is considered most perilous. If the hungry ghosts devour the ancestral spirits of the deceased, then all succeeding generations will cease to exist.'"

Cassidy felt the room begin to spin. "So, he's going to get my ancestors to come to him by sacrificing me!" she said. She forced herself to stay calm, to think. There was something that didn't add up. "Wait, no, James," she said, "You said that he couldn't do that. The coins can't be taken, remember? If he killed me, he would still be taking them!"

"Not you," James said softly.

"But who..." Cassidy began. Then she realized what James was trying to tell her. She gasped and gripped the table.

"My dad!"

❧ Chapter Twenty-Two

Cassidy's ears began to ring, and her vision darkened to a narrow pinpoint of light. She thought for a moment that she was going to faint.

"Take a deep breath, Cassidy," James said. "Just breathe."

James moved closer to Cassidy and placed his hand on her back. The warmth of his touch soothed her, and she wanted to lean against him and let him hold her. *No, you have to pull yourself together,* she told herself. *You have to figure this out!*

Cassidy continued to take deep breaths and

tried to calm her mind. A piercing shriek startled her, and her head whipped around toward the sound. A black form clung to the window and peered in at Cassidy. It was moving its mouth as if it was trying to speak.

James followed Cassidy's eyes to the window, but she knew he wasn't seeing what she saw—the shrieking black ghost pressing itself to the glass. She listened to the sound that came from its rounded open mouth. The high-pitched howl seemed to be vibrating on some level beyond normal spoken language.

She knew that it was definitely trying to communicate. Was it threatening her? Demanding something? She forced herself to concentrate on the shrill sounds. Finally she made out several syllables and repeated them to James. He stared at her, confused.

"Did you understand that?" she asked him. "Do you know what the words mean?"

"Yeah," he said. "You just said a phrase in Mandarin. You said, 'Where's the sixth coin?'"

Cassidy looked at James. "You mean the fifth coin?" she asked.

But James shook his head. "No, you definitely said, 'Where's the sixth coin?'"

Cassidy turned back to the window, but the hungry ghost had disappeared.

"What's this all about, Cass?" James asked.

"How do you know Mandarin?"

"The hungry ghost at the window—it was sort of screaming those words at me. But what's it supposed to mean, James? There's no sixth coin!" Cassidy felt the flat silk pouch against her skin beneath her shirt. *There are only five coins, so why did the ghost ask about a sixth?*

"I don't know, but I think we better get out of here. Mr. Perkins is gonna be waiting for us." James stood up and placed the book back on the cart.

"But we have to figure this out," Cassidy said, feeling the panic rise inside her. "My dad could be in danger! We have to find him!"

James guided Cassidy quickly to the elevators. "Let's get back to the hotel," he said. "Maybe your dad is back by now. If he's not, we'll try to find a number for your cousin. Don't worry, Cass. He's gonna be okay."

But Cassidy could hear doubt in James's voice. As the elevator descended the five floors to the main lobby, Cassidy felt that she was falling into a dark hole of despair with no hope of ever finding her way out.

@@@@@

By the time the elevator doors opened, Cassidy had gotten her runaway emotions under control, and she and James began working out a plan. "We have to find Master Lau," Cassidy said. "We need to know what he's doing, where he's going."

They walked over to a beautiful indoor fountain at the front of the museum to wait for Mr. Perkins. Tourists and schoolchildren in neat uniforms milled around the entrance, and they had to talk quietly to avoid being overheard.

"I think it's kind of strange that Lau hasn't been around much since we got to Hong Kong. Have you noticed? At practice yesterday he was zoning out, and then he wasn't at dinner last night at all," James said. "The chaperones are the ones who are taking the groups out to the activities today."

"Yeah," said Cassidy. "So where is he? You think he's doing something with the other *shifus* from Seattle? I heard Shifu Karder say that they were going on some tour today."

"I seriously doubt it," James said. "He didn't seem to be too friendly with any of the other teachers."

Then Cassidy had a frightening thought. "You think he followed my dad? Dad's cousin picked him up, and they were going out to visit some relatives somewhere."

"I'm sure your dad's okay," James said, and put his hand on her arm reassuringly. "He's with his cousin. I doubt Master Lau would make any kind of move if your dad had somebody with him."

Cassidy nodded. "Yeah, I guess you're right," she said. His hand on her arm felt warm and comforting.

Just then a Chinese woman who looked to be in her midthirties exited one of the elevators and raised her hand in a wave. "Excuse me, James? James Tang?" she called.

As James looked toward the woman Cassidy saw a look of uncertainty cross his face.

"James, you don't remember me," the woman said. "You were just a young boy when I saw you last."

But Cassidy could see that he did recognize the pretty woman with the warm smile. He let her take both of his hands in hers. "I'm Ting-lan, your mother's sister," she said.

"You look . . ." Cassidy noticed that James paused and then cleared his throat. "You look so much like my mother," he said at last.

Ting-lan beamed. "What a wonderful thing to hear!" she said. "Your mother was one of the most beautiful women I've ever seen."

"Yeah," James said softly. "She was."

"And are you James's girlfriend?" Ting-lan said, beaming at Cassidy.

"Uh . . . no," Cassidy stammered, and blushed deeply. "I'm Cassidy Chen," she said. "We're here for the kung fu tournament."

Cassidy noticed that James was trying to hide a grin. *Is he laughing at me?* Cassidy wondered.

"Ahh, still a Wing Chun star, then," Ting-lan said. "James, your mother was so proud of you. She was always saying, 'James has taken first certificate' in this or that."

Cassidy noticed the name tag on the lapel of Ting-lan's smart blue suit. "So you work here at the museum?" she asked.

"Yes, I work in outreach services for the museum," she said. "I always see your father when he comes to the museum for work. He tells me what you're up to."

James looked momentarily stunned. Cassidy guessed that his father had never mentioned seeing James's aunt on any of his trips.

Ting-lan must have sensed the same thing. "Ahh, so you've heard nothing about me, then," she said. "It doesn't surprise me. Your father is always courteous and very proper when he asks about our family, but he doesn't want to talk about Li Wei."

"Yeah, that sounds like Dad," James said. "I think that's why he moved us to the States so soon . . . so soon after it happened."

"I admired your mother so much, James," Ting-lan said. "She was a few years older than me and so much fun! I don't know if you remember, but your dad was different then, too. She helped him to enjoy life."

James looked down at the green marble floor and paused before speaking. "Yeah," he said softly, and looked up at the woman who looked so much like his mother. "I kind of remember what it was like then."

"You'll have to come and visit me before you go home," Ting-lan said, handing him her business card. "Bring Cassidy, too. Will you do that?"

"Sure," James said.

Cassidy nodded, thrilled that he wanted to include her. She tried to push the terrifying uncertainty of her future out of her mind.

"Oh, James," Ting-lan said, and leaned in closer to put her arm around him. "I knew your mother better than anyone else, and I know that she would be so happy that you're here in China. She would want you to enjoy life, as she did."

Cassidy saw James nod his head slightly, and then he looked at Ting-lan. "Yeah, you're right," he said to her. "That's exactly what she would want."

"Then promise me, for your mother's sake, that you will do just that," Ting-lan said. "Promise me."

"Okay, I promise," James said to her, laughing.

Ting-lan looked at Cassidy and smiled. "You

are a witness," she said. "You heard James's promise. Please report to me if he breaks it!"

"I will," Cassidy said. "But I doubt that James would break a promise to anyone."

❀ *Chapter Twenty-Three*

Back at the hotel Cassidy saw that the groups were just returning with their chaperones. But Master Lau wasn't there, and neither was her father.

The students were told that there would be a shopping expedition leaving in the afternoon. After that they would all go and watch the preparations for the Hungry Ghost Festival.

"Are you okay, James?" Cassidy asked. He had been very quiet since meeting his aunt.

"Yeah," he said. "I really am. She just looked so much like my mother, you know?"

"Yeah, I know," Cassidy said. "I mean, I know it must have seemed strange—but probably good, too. Right?" James nodded and awkwardly started to reach for Cassidy's hand, but then dropped it as Majesta strolled up to them.

"Have fun?" Majesta asked. "In a boring old museum with boring old stuff everywhere?"

"Yeah," James said, giving Cassidy a quick smile. "I kind of like boring old museums." Cassidy wondered if he would tell Majesta about seeing his mother's sister in the museum. Somehow she doubted it.

"What about you, Majesta?" Cassidy asked. "How was the boat ride?"

Majesta flipped her hair back, her picture-perfect face glowing from the sun and wind. "It was amazing," she said. "The water was so blue, and there were all these little markets built right next to the water. I bought some gorgeous silk scarves and the cutest little ceramic dragon. And we had this fantastic view of the mountains. A boat tour is definitely the way to go! We got to see everything!"

Cassidy thought about the hungry ghosts that were roaming the city. Majesta had definitely not seen everything.

"I need to run up to the room," Majesta said. "I want to grab some more money before we go shopping later. Wanna come with?" she asked Cassidy.

Cassidy glanced over at James, wishing they'd had a chance to talk about their plan for the rest of the day.

"Ah, yeah, I'll go with you," Cassidy said, figuring that if Majesta was trying to be friendly, the least she could do was to return the favor.

"I'll head up to my room, too," James said. "Then we can meet back in the lobby."

Cassidy tried to catch James's attention in the elevator, but Majesta was still talking about the boat trip, the stops they'd made along the way, and what she'd bought, without giving Cassidy or James a chance to get a word in.

When the elevator doors opened, Majesta stepped off first and fumbled in her bag for the room key. James leaned in close to Cassidy and whispered, "Meet me in half an hour."

They had been told to meet in the lobby in an hour for the shopping expedition. This would give them some time to figure out what they needed to do before leaving with the rest of the group. Cassidy nodded quickly and then followed Majesta and her shopping bags down the hall to their room.

The red light on the telephone was flashing when Cassidy and Majesta walked in to their room. "A message!" Majesta squealed. She quickly dialed the front desk and gave the desk clerk their room number. A look of disappointment crossed Majesta's face. "Yeah, she's here. Hold on," she said. "I think I'll take a quick shower," Majesta said to Cassidy as she gave her the phone. "They're taking us to some really nice fashion shops, and I plan to try on lots of clothes!"

"Hello?" Cassidy said into the phone, wondering who would have called.

"This is the front desk," a clipped, British voice said. "Your mother left a message and asked you to call her at home. She said to tell you that it's not an emergency; she just wishes to speak to you."

Cassidy's heart beat faster, even though she had just been told it was not an emergency. They had agreed before Simon and Cassidy left for Hong Kong that they would not call each other in order to save the expense of long-distance telephone charges. Cassidy had read in the hotel brochure that an Internet café downstairs allowed guests to send e-mail for free. She knew her dad had sent her mom an e-mail soon after they arrived, letting her know they had arrived safely. *So why is Mom calling?*

🌸 Chapter Twenty-Four

Cassidy read the small laminated card next to the phone that gave instructions for making international calls. She punched in the long series of digits and waited to hear her mother's voice. *Please don't let anything be wrong!* she thought over and over as she waited.

"Hello?" Wendy Chen answered.

"Hey, Mom," Cassidy said, wondering if her voice sounded shaky across the thousands of miles to Seattle. "The desk said you called."

"Oh, Cassidy!" her mom said. "It's so good to

hear your voice. I've missed you so much!"

"Mom," Cassidy said, relaxing a little. "I've only been gone, like, less than forty-eight hours. And Dad e-mailed you when we got here."

"I know, honey," her mom said. "And I got the e-mail. But it's just . . ."

Cassidy heard the hesitation in her mother's voice. She went on alert again. There was something that her mom wasn't saying.

"What is it, Mom?" Cassidy asked. "You sound kind of funny. Is something wrong?"

Cassidy heard the white noise that fills the void in telephone calls, especially long-distance telephone calls. "Mom?" Cassidy said, feeling a sense of panic begin to rise within her.

"Cassidy, is everything all right there?" her mother said at last. "Are you okay? Is your dad okay?"

What does Mom know? Why is she asking me this?

"Uh, yeah, Mom," Cassidy said, glancing at Majesta, who was obviously listening to the conversation. Majesta grinned and then silently mouthed the word *mothers*! She took a fluffy white robe from the hook next to the door and went into the bathroom.

"This is so silly," Cassidy's mother said with an embarrassed laugh. "I can't believe I called you. We said that we wouldn't call."

"It's okay, Mom," Cassidy told her. "But you got me kind of worried. Is everything all right?"

"You're going to think this is ridiculous, but okay, I'll tell you." Cassidy could hear her mother take a deep breath and let it out again. "When I got back from dropping you off at the airport, I walked into the house and it was filled, and I mean *filled*, with a really strong lavender scent."

Cassidy remembered the first time that her Irish great-grandmother had appeared to her as a spirit. Later, after she had disappeared, Cassidy's mother walked into the room. She had sniffed the air and asked, "Can you smell lavender? That scent always reminds me of my grandmother."

"Maybe you had the windows open, Mom, or . . ." Cassidy began, but her mother interrupted her.

"Yes, the windows were open, but there's no lavender growing around here. The scent was very strong, Cassidy, and I could smell it in every room of the house."

Did the spirit of my great-grandmother Fiona visit my mom? But why?

"But that's not all, Cass," Wendy said, and Cassidy noticed that her mother's voice had grown softer. It was almost a whisper now. Cassidy pressed the heavy black telephone receiver closer to her ear.

"Today I walked into the living room," her

mother said, "and the rocking chair near the front window was . . ."

Cassidy felt a chill run down her spine as her mother paused to find the words to describe what she saw. "It was rocking slowly back and forth. Steady and deliberately. Like somebody was sitting in it."

"It was probably just Monty," said Cassidy. But before she could suggest that her cat had probably jumped down from the chair, her mother said, "And then I heard a voice. It was very soft, but I heard it. It . . . it was my grandmother's voice. I'd recognize her Irish lilt anywhere."

Cassidy found that she was staring at the green and beige floral print on the bed, the colors swirling before her eyes as she listened to her mother's disembodied voice across the miles.

"What did she say, Mom?" Cassidy asked.

"She said, 'Call your beautiful, sweet daughter. Tell her that you love her.'"

Cassidy gripped the phone, listening to the crackling line between them. She didn't know what to say, what any of this meant.

Her mother broke the silence. "It was the way she said it, Cass. Her voice sounded sad, I think. I tried to just ignore the whole thing. I thought I was being emotional and sentimental, so I put it out of my head. But this morning I got up and I realized I just had to call. I had to hear your voice and know that you were okay." Her mother gave an odd little laugh. "This is crazy, I know."

"No, Mom, I don't think it's crazy at all. I think it's nice. I'm glad you called. And I love you, too," Cassidy said, her voice catching. She felt a pressure behind her eyes, and she fought back the tears.

"I'm sure it's just because the house feels so empty," her mom said. "This is the first time we've really been away from each other, and I miss you so much."

"Sure, Mom," Cassidy said, willing herself to remain calm so that her mother couldn't hear the fear in her voice. "That's probably all it was."

After they said good-bye, Cassidy put the telephone back on the receiver and walked over to the large window. She stared out across the bright sky of Hong Kong to the mountains in the distance.

Cassidy longed for her mother. She longed to wrap herself in her mother's arms the way she used to when she was little and had had a nightmare. But this was no nightmare, and she would not be running into the safety of her mother's arms this time. This was real life. And Cassidy knew in her heart the reason that Great-grandmother Fiona had visited her mom. *She knows that I might not make it through this last battle. She wanted to give my mother one last chance to say good-bye.*

❧ Chapter Twenty-Five

Majesta was still in the shower when Cassidy left the room to meet James. He stood waiting near the panel of revolving glass doors and didn't notice her until she was at his side.

"Hey you," she said, still shaken by the phone call from her mother.

James looked down at her and smiled. His smile was something that Cassidy would never get tired of seeing. That and the slightly messy way his hair fell across his forehead. For a moment Cassidy felt like putting her face against his shoulder and crying, but she could not give in to her emotions. That wouldn't help her right now. *I need to be strong. I need the calm warrior's mind to figure this out*, she told herself. *If I have to have a meltdown, I'll do it later, when this is all over.* A sudden cold sweat reminded Cassidy that, for her, there might not be a later.

"Have you seen Master Lau?" Cassidy asked James.

"No," James said. "I called up to his room when we got back from the museum. I had a question about the tournament all ready in case he answered, but he didn't. So I came straight down here, and I've been watching the doors ever since. There's been no sign of him. No one else seems to have seen him, either."

"Where could he be? Do you think he's at the tournament site?" Cassidy asked.

"No," James said grimly. "I don't think he's even thinking about the tournament at all. My guess is that he's somewhere planning his next move, calling up evil spirits or something."

"Ms. Chen?" a voice called across the wide marble expanse of lobby.

Cassidy glanced toward the front desk. A receptionist dressed in a black-and-white uniform held a piece of paper in his hand and motioned her over.

"You just missed a call from your father. You

must have been on your way downstairs." He handed a folded slip of cream-colored stationery to Cassidy.

I'm spending the day with Stephen and having dinner with his family tonight. I'll catch up with you tomorrow morning before the tournament begins. Love, Dad.

Cassidy frowned and gave the note to James. "I guess that might be good," she said. "I mean, I'd rather know that he's with his cousins than here in the city."

James checked the large, gold-framed clock above the registration desk. "Look, we don't have much time before the others get down here," he told her. "I want to look for Lau. If we know where he is, then we'll be able to protect you and your dad better."

"But James, he could be anywhere," Cassidy pointed out. "Nobody's seen him."

"I think he might be in one of the shops in this district a few blocks away. We know he's involved in dark magic, and there's this old section of Hong Kong where you can buy just about anything."

"Do we have time?" Cassidy asked.

"Not we," James told her. "Just me. You stay here and watch the doors. See if he comes in."

"No," Cassidy protested. "I don't think that's a good idea. We shouldn't get separated."

"I know where I'm going, Cass," James told her. "I've checked the map. And remember, I used to live here. My mom and I used to visit her cousin down there." Cassidy heard a confidence in his voice that she hadn't heard before when he talked of his mother.

"I won't be gone long," he promised as he started across the lobby. "Just stay here and wait for me."

Before she could say another word, James was out the door. She lost sight of him in the sea of pedestrians on the sidewalk.

Cassidy still held her father's note in her hand. She read the words again, thankful that he was with his relatives. *He's probably having a great time,* she thought. *I bet he's asking them a million questions about our ancestors so he can finish his family chart.* She could see her father taking notes and showing his cousins the old photographs he had brought with him.

But my grandfather, she worried. *Where is he right now? Is he safe? Does he know what's going on?*

Then a new thought chilled her. What if the relative Master Lau planned to sacrifice wasn't her father, but her grandfather? *No,* she thought, pushing the idea from her mind. *No one knows he's alive. Everyone thinks he drowned all those years ago.*

Car horns suddenly blared out in the street. Traffic had come to yet another dead stop, and the frustrated drivers joined in the noisy chaos of Hong

Kong traffic. Cassidy glanced toward the commotion and found herself looking into the face of the man who had handed her the wooden box of coins almost a year before.

Her grandfather!

❧ Chapter Twenty-Six

For a moment Cassidy froze with confusion and surprise. The instant she looked into his eyes, she knew that it was her grandfather. But just as quickly as he had appeared, he disappeared into the crowd. Cassidy pushed through the revolving door, trying to keep her eyes on the back of his white shirt as he moved through the throngs.

At one point, he slowed down as he took a right turn between two buildings, and Cassidy thought she might be able to catch up to him. He slipped into an alley lined with souvenir shops, each small booth illuminated with strings of colored lights. Her heart racing, Cassidy pushed past the crowds of tourists, ignoring the shopkeepers who called out to her. *I can't let him get away,* she thought. *I have to warn him about Master Lau!*

As her grandfather quickly exited the narrow path between the buildings, he glanced back over his shoulder toward Cassidy and then turned left. He was no more than fifty or sixty feet ahead of her, but shoppers jammed the distance between them. Cassidy struggled to keep him in her sight.

When she made the turn and followed him down a narrow, winding street, she knew that she had entered a different part of Hong Kong than the bustling, modern area where they were staying.

The tightly packed buildings cast long shadows, and the streets were lit by small, flickering iron lamps attached to wooden posts. They cast a series of pale yellowish pools of light on the pavement below. Cassidy also noticed that there weren't as many people around. The people who were out on the street all seemed to be heading in the same direction—the opposite of the way she was going—talking and laughing with one another and carrying woven baskets and canvas bags of what looked like fruit and candy.

Cassidy strained to keep her eyes trained on her grandfather's back. He was weaving in and out of the crowd of people, but he didn't seem to be in a hurry. *Does he want me to catch up to him?* she wondered. She found herself swept along with the crowd of men, women, and children, all clearly in a festive mood.

Ahead of her she saw that the narrow street opened into a large, empty intersection. Strangely, there was no traffic on the street, only people. Cassidy looked around and saw that the streets that fed into the intersection had been roped off.

A pulsing drumbeat began, like low, faraway thunder at first, then it rose in volume and intensity until Cassidy felt that it matched her own pounding heartbeat. She darted between the families, who were pushing in closer now. She couldn't lose her grandfather!

Where is he? Cassidy squinted through the crowd and the shimmering streetlights to find him. She dashed toward a man wearing a white shirt, but when he turned, she realized that it wasn't her grandfather at all, but a much younger man.

Where had he gone? She scanned the faces, hoping to spot her grandfather. *Did he get away?*

Cassidy was jostled as the crowd parted. Several men pushed a large wagon into the center of the courtyard. Standing atop the wooden platform of the wagon was a towering fifteen-foot figure made of bamboo and small squares of colored paper. The massive head of the figure looked like it was made of papier mâché, and the face was shaped into a fierce scowl. Its glassy, cruel eyes stared out over the crowd. Cassidy noticed a college-age girl standing near her with several of her friends. She hoped that someone in the group could speak English.

"Who is that supposed to be?" Cassidy asked the girl, practically shouting to be heard over the roar of the crowd.

The girl laughed, then said, "King of the Underworld. We're going to burn him at midnight in a big bonfire. It's for the Hungry Ghost Festival!"

"But I thought that started tomorrow," Cassidy said. She had seen the posters in the hotel, and she knew that it said the festival would start the following day, even though the street vendors would set up their tables tonight.

The girl laughed again. "That's for the tourists. It's a big joke. They sell lots of Hungry Ghost souvenirs! Make lots of money!"

Another girl who had been listening to their conversation leaned in to be heard. "This is the real thing," she said. "At midnight tonight the underworld is opened! We're throwing food to the king so that when the hungry ghosts come, they will eat the treats and not our souls!"

The girl pointed, and Cassidy saw that several of the children near the front of the crowd were throwing oranges, peaches, and small handfuls of wrapped candy at the feet of the menacing figure, squealing when they hit their mark.

Cassidy's heart thudded faster. *That means Master Lau is planning the sacrifice for tonight! Time really has run out!*

The steady drumbeats intensified, and above the thunderous roar Cassidy heard a gong. The resounding ring echoed around the buildings that faced the small courtyard. Then the loud, mournful sound of reed pipes rose in a sorrowful melody above the boisterous crowd and hung in the darkness over their heads.

Cassidy turned to ask the girls more questions, but they had moved away from her and joined another group of young people. She peered through the crowds and didn't see her grandfather anywhere. She had lost him. *My one opportunity to warn him about Master Lau and to ask him about the coins is gone.*

She began to work her way out of the crowd. At the edge of the group, she noticed that several tables had been set up. She saw the glowing tips of hundreds of incense sticks, each one sending a fragrant, curling plume of smoke into the night.

She looked all around and wondered how she could get back to the hotel. Nothing looked familiar. She had been so focused on following her grandfather that she hadn't paid attention to the streets.

"Excuse me," she said to a woman holding a young child in her arms. "Can you tell me how to get back to the Victoria Harbor Hotel?"

The woman shook her head to indicate that she didn't understand English.

Cassidy had to get back to the hotel. James would probably be back by now. She hadn't watched the door for Master Lau as they had planned, but he would understand that she had to try to find her grandfather.

The fear nearly overcame Cassidy as the sound of the pulsing music continued to pound inside her head. *I have to get back. I have to get back to the hotel, to James.*

Beyond the crowded street, the rest of the area lay in peculiar shadows. The odd angles of the old buildings seemed almost threatening and defied any sense of order. *Nothing looks familiar. How am I going to get back?*

Cassidy looked for the girls she had talked to earlier, but they were lost in the colorful crowd of people that circled the King of the Underworld. She thought about the shrine back in her hotel room and longed to touch the smooth leaves of jade and gold. *Please help me*, she silently called out to her ancestors. *I know you can help me find my way back!*

Suddenly someone pushed a cloth in front of her nose. A damp, musty odor like mushrooms filled her senses. At the same time, her vision began to blur. The swirling colors of the festival merged like an oily mix of paint sliding down the canvas of night.

Just before her eyes closed, she felt the rough cloth of a hood being pulled over her head, and then everything turned to black.

❀ Chapter Twenty-Seven

When Cassidy awoke, her eyes felt filmy, and she had to blink several times to clear her vision. At first she thought that she was in her room and that she'd just had a weird dream. She was even thinking about how she would describe it to James. *I was at the Festival of Hungry Ghosts and I was lost, and I really started to panic because I didn't know how to find my way back—but then . . .*

Cassidy sat up quickly when she remembered what had happened next. *The earthy smelling cloth. The hood over my head!* Someone had drugged her and kidnapped her!

Cassidy looked around and found that she was in a large, open room made of stone. Most of the roof and some of the walls were gone, and she could see through to the starry night above. She had the startling sensation that she was high up on a hilltop or mountain, far from the city. Fiery torchlights like orange and yellow phantoms cast demonic, dancing shadows against the stones. *Where am I? What is this place?*

Then Cassidy realized with a sickening horror that she wasn't alone. She'd heard just the slightest sound, no more than the brush of cloth against stone. But her senses were heightened, and she knew beyond a doubt that *someone* was in the room with her, watching her.

She searched the dark corners with her eyes as she slowly rose to her feet. She needed to be ready to strike. Then her eyes fell on the figure of a man sitting with his back against the opposite wall. She could just make out his shadowy outline, but she couldn't see his face.

Her kidnapper!

"I see you," she said, her voice quavering. She was on her feet now, but her legs still felt weak and her head fuzzy from whatever he had drugged her with. *Can I even fight?* She wasn't sure at that moment that she had the strength to face whoever sat across the room from her. *Can it be Master Lau?*

The man stood and stepped toward her. Cassidy's body instinctively went into a kung fu stance.

"Don't come any closer!" she ordered, attempting to put as much force behind her words as possible. But even to Cassidy's own ears, her voice sounded thin and frightened.

"Don't be afraid." The man's voice was familiar to Cassidy, but it sounded far away, as if he were speaking through water. She felt that she was moving through fog as she took a step back to get away from the dark figure across the room.

The man took a step closer. Cassidy backed up again and suddenly felt the cold stones of the wall through her sweatshirt. She heard the slight metallic jingle of the coins in the silk pouch around her waist.

"Who are you?" she demanded. Just at that moment the man stepped into the large square of orange flickering light from the torches that burned outside. In that ghostly illumination Cassidy saw who he was. Her grandfather.

She had been kidnapped by her own grandfather? The confusion and lingering effects of whatever drug was still coursing through her bloodstream were overwhelming. Cassidy staggered forward once and then stumbled backward. She hit hard against the wall behind her and felt the air rush from her lungs. She watched her grandfather moving through the shadows toward her. The room began to spin with the unearthly orange glow. Cassidy closed her eyes just before she fell to the cold stone floor.

❧ Chapter Twenty-Eight

"Mingmei, look at me! This will help you!" Cassidy's eyes fluttered open once, then twice as she tried to keep her heavy lids open. She willed herself to focus on the face in front of her. "Mingmei, I am your grandfather. I'm here to help you. Please don't be afraid."

Cassidy took a deep, ragged breath as she tried to understand what he was saying. "Who . . . why did you . . ." Her speech felt slurred, her tongue thick.

Her grandfather opened a soft white cloth and removed several small leaves. Cassidy's eyes were beginning to clear in the near darkness of the stone room. She watched closely as her grandfather crushed the leaves between his fingers, and then he rubbed them into his palm.

"This will help you," her grandfather said as he held his open palm up to her face. "Take a deep breath of this and then exhale. The leaves will cleanse your muddy thoughts."

But Cassidy wasn't sure if she could trust him. He was the one who had drugged her in the first place! She could tell he sensed her hesitation.

"Please, Mingmei, we don't have much time and there's much to tell. You need to have a clear head for what is to come. For who is to come!"

As soon as he said the words, Cassidy felt certain that she knew who her grandfather meant. Master Lau! She leaned into her grandfather's palm and took a deep breath of the crushed leaves.

Instantly she felt a cool, mint-scented rush enter her body. The sensation felt wonderful, and she breathed as deeply as she could to take in as much of the refreshing odor as possible. As she exhaled she felt cleansed, as if all her cloudy thoughts and confused ideas washed away and dissolved into the night.

Her grandfather sat back and wiped his hands together, the crushed leaves falling to the floor between them. "Do you feel better?" he asked her.

"Yeah, I think so," Cassidy said. "What was

the other stuff? It smelled like mushrooms." Now that her mind was clear she had many questions, and it appeared that her grandfather was the only one who might be able to answer them.

"The other was an oil that I extracted from a plant that grows here in China," he explained. "I wouldn't have used it if there had been any other way. Please believe me, it is safe, except for the somewhat fuzzy mind that you have upon waking."

"But why did you drug me?" Cassidy asked.

"I couldn't risk any sort of disturbance or take the time to answer questions. I thought that this way was best. But I'm deeply sorry that you were frightened."

"I was following you," Cassidy said. "I saw you outside the hotel, and I was trying to catch up to you. Why did you run away from me?"

Cassidy was certain that she saw the faintest flicker of a grin cross her grandfather's otherwise very serious face. "I didn't run away from you, little Mingmei," he said. "I was actually leading you away from the hotel. You were being watched, and I couldn't risk approaching you until I knew that we had lost whoever—or whatever—was keeping an eye on you. I had to wait until I felt it was safe."

So he did want me to catch him, Cassidy thought, remembering how at times he had seemed to slow down and wait for her to catch up.

"How did you carry me all the way up this mountain?" she asked.

"I disguised myself as a monk and used one of their utility carts to transport you." He pointed to an old wooden cart that was covered with a blanket and a dark robe. "I didn't want anyone who might be watching to know it was me."

"Grandfather." She said the word tentatively, and it sounded odd on her tongue. She could see that it pleased him. "I still don't understand. I was trying to find you so that I could warn you about Master Lau — about what James and I think he plans to do."

Her grandfather sighed deeply, and his eyes darkened with worry. "So you and your friend have figured out that evil man's plan, then?"

"Most of it, I think," Cassidy said. "He wants the coins, right?"

A sad smile tugged at the corners of her grandfather's mouth. "The coins," he repeated. "For fifty years Chiu Chi Lau has burned to own those coins. I'm afraid it has consumed his life."

"What does he want to do with them?" Cassidy asked. She thought about the five unusual coins, each imprisoning the spirit of a long-ago defeated enemy.

Grandfather Li shook his head slightly, and Cassidy noticed the white streak, featherlike against his dark hair.

"I'm afraid it's difficult to understand obsession,

my granddaughter. But from the first moment that he laid eyes on the coins, when they were in my possession, he wanted them. I can only guess at his ultimate intention, but I think he wants to harness their power with his dark magic. Perhaps he believes the coins will make him stronger, and possibly even immortal. As I said, it's difficult to understand the obsessive mind of a mad man."

"He's really, really bad, Grandfather," Cassidy said, and realized how natural the name felt. "I saw him do some kind of evil ceremony. He was calling up dark spirits."

"Yes," he said. "I'm aware of what he's been up to. I've been keeping an eye on him, and you, since your fourteenth birthday."

He's been keeping an eye on me? All this time? She remembered that her dad's mother had sometimes thought her husband's spirit was around, watching over them, when she would find white feathers. She felt comforted to know that he had been looking out for her.

"The spirits you saw him call out were, indeed, some of the early hungry ghosts. Soulless, very sad, very troublesome. They can cause many problems. He gave them early entry into the world, but he found that he couldn't control them."

"But why was he calling them out at all? Isn't tonight at midnight when they're all released?" Cassidy asked. "What was he trying to do by calling out any of the ghosts early?"

"He was experimenting, you might say," her grandfather explained. "He was trying to find some particularly nasty—and very powerful—ghosts to help him with his plan."

Cassidy's insides trembled as she realized the kind of harm the really evil and powerful hungry ghosts might do. But something about this still didn't make sense. *How would the ghosts help him with his plan?*

"James and I figured out that he can't actually take the coins from me," Cassidy said. "We also figured out that he can't kill me and take them, because that would sort of be the same . . ."

"Yes, that's correct," her grandfather explained. "I've spent almost my entire life doing as much research as I could to figure out what the coins mean and what your destiny is all about. Even before you were born! As the first female descended from both Ng Mui and her friend Wing Chun, the coins are yours now, in life and in death."

"So then why, Grandfather? If the evil ghosts can't kill me, then how does Master Lau plan to use them?" Cassidy asked.

"That's very easy to answer, Mingmei," her grandfather said. "He knows that you will fight to protect someone you love. He knows that your skills and abilities—and powers—far exceed his. He needs the evil hungry ghosts as his protection against you! If it comes down to a fight, then he wants to weigh the odds in his favor. He's afraid to fight you alone."

Afraid, Cassidy thought with some satisfaction. *Master Lau is afraid of me.*

"Well, he should be afraid," she said fiercely. "Because I will fight him. I'll fight him to the death if he tries to hurt anyone I love."

"Now do you understand why he needs the evil ghosts? Their purpose is to keep you out of Lau's way while he carries out his wicked plan."

"My friend James and I think that he's planning a sacrifice," said Cassidy.

"I think you're right. Lau intends to offer up one of your relatives in death in order to draw your ancestors together," her grandfather said. "When that happens at midnight tonight, just as the gates of the underworld are opened, millions of dark, lost, starving, wandering souls will also be here. These hungry ghosts will devour the light-filled and truly loved spirits of those who came before you."

"And if that were to actually happen, which it won't," Cassidy vowed, "the spirits of my ancestors would be devoured and I would cease to exist. And that's when the coins would be his."

"That's correct," her grandfather said.

"So is that why we're hiding up here?" Cassidy asked. "Because if he can't find you to kill you, then the ancestors won't gather and the hungry ghosts won't be drawn to them."

Her grandfather looked confused for a moment. "It's not me," he said. "Chiu Chi Lau doesn't even know that I'm alive. He thought that I drowned many years ago when Simon was just a young boy."

"He doesn't know about you?" Cassidy asked. A dark and icy feeling gripped her heart as she realized her greatest fear was coming true.

"He is after your father, Mingmei," Grandfather Li said solemnly. "Chiu Chi Lau has planned to kidnap him with the help of the very powerful hungry ghosts. In fact, it may have already happened. If so, then they are on their way up here right now."

 Chapter Twenty-Nine

As Cassidy let her grandfather's terrifying words sink in, she began to feel as if the stone walls were closing in on her.

"I need to go outside," she told her grandfather in a rush of words and breath.

He escorted her through the low opening and stood beside her as she gulped the night air, willing herself to be calm. *I have to do something. I can't let this happen!* She pictured the tranquil pool of water, and one by one she pushed aside the negative, worrying, runaway thoughts.

Finally she was calm enough to look around. She knew that she needed to get her bearings, to figure out where she was and what was around her. She wanted to have the best advantage before Master Lau and the evil ghosts arrived with her father.

The first thing she noticed was that they were very high above the city. The lights of Hong Kong looked like tiny pinpricks in the darkness far below them. She saw shimmering lights out on the water in the far distance.

Then she checked out her immediate surroundings. She and her grandfather stood in a clearing made of hard-packed earth just outside the ruins of an ancient temple. Tall, heavy poles stood as sentinels around the stone walls of the temple, and an eternal flame burned in a clay bowl atop each one. Some of the walls were still standing, but others had toppled over in a heap of jagged stones. There was a still and solemn feeling in the clearing at the top of the mountain. Cassidy sensed that the stone walls had witnessed much sadness, and maybe even violence.

"Master Lau picked this place for a reason, didn't he?" Cassidy asked her grandfather.

"Yes, I think so," he said. "I've been following him for some time, and I know that he feels this ground is sacred to his evil cause. Hundreds of years ago many faithful monks were killed here. They were attempting to protect their temple from a band of savage invaders.

The torches are kept lit in their memory. I think that Lau probably sees this as a place where evil won out over good."

Cassidy thought about this, and it made perfect sense — or at least it would in the mind of the evil and deeply disturbed Chiu Chi Lau.

"How do you know he's kidnapped my dad?" she asked. "My father had plans to spend the day with his cousin. We thought he'd be safe . . ." Her voice trailed off.

"Once Lau arrived in Hong Kong, he went straight to the shop of a known spiritualist of the dark side. After that I followed him to an empty warehouse near the docks. I observed the ceremony he performed there, and I realized that this time he knew what he was doing."

"So you saw him call up the ghosts?" Cassidy asked. "And you figured out that he plans to use them to kidnap my father. Why didn't you stop him then?"

"Mingmei, you must understand, the prophecy will unfold as it is intended. That is something that I have learned. You are the only one who can change the course. Because of this I felt it was more important to follow you and then bring you up here so that you could be ready for what is to come. Together we will fight for Simon once Lau arrives."

Cassidy realized that her grandfather was right. Just as her ancestors first told her, she couldn't run from or change this destiny.

"So, this ceremony that you saw," Cassidy said. "You said that now he knows what he's doing, right? Does that mean that he's got some really powerful ghosts on his side—ghosts that he can actually control?"

"Yes," her grandfather said softly. "There are three of them, and they are very powerful demons. Lau has promised them much if the ghosts will do his bidding. That's how he is able to control them this time."

"And you think they've already taken my dad?" Cassidy asked.

"I imagine so. I heard him instructing the ghosts before I left him to follow you. He intended to tell your father that you'd been in an accident and that he would accompany him to the hospital."

"So you think they're on their way here now?" Cassidy asked, peering out through the darkness beyond the flickering orange flames of the torches.

"Yes, I'm sure of it. He needs to have Simon up here before midnight. They will be on foot and the path is overgrown, so it will be a slow trip for them. He planned to have the three demons disguise themselves as men."

"My father must know by now that they're not on the way to a hospital to see me." Cassidy said. "He must be frantic!"

Cassidy felt an overwhelming urge to storm down the side of the mountain and face Lau and the three hungry ghost demons that minute. Her blood ran hot in her veins, and she felt a throbbing pulse at her temple. But she knew that she needed to keep a cool head. She needed a plan, and for that she needed more information.

"What are we facing, Grandfather?" Cassidy asked. Her teeth clenched in anger at the thought of what her father must be going through right now. "Exactly who and what am I going to be fighting?"

Grandfather Li watched Cassidy's face carefully before he spoke. "The three ghosts hunger for evil. They thirst for the opportunity to make others suffer. I believe that Lau has finally succeeded in calling up demons more powerful than any of the demons you've battled in the past, Mingmei."

Cassidy's thoughts raced. *I can't do this! Somehow I'm supposed to be able to* . . . She stopped and remembered that she could control these negative thoughts that would get her nowhere.

"Grandfather, I need to spend a few minutes alone," Cassidy said. She wished that she had her warrior's shrine with her now. The battle was near. The enemy was on its way and she had to be ready.

Grandfather Li bowed his head slightly. "I understand. All we can do now is wait. I will watch the path."

He walked away from Cassidy to the other side of the clearing. She noticed that he stood still and straight as he watched and listened for his old enemy from his boyhood—the man who planned to kill his beloved son and destroy his entire line of ancestors.

Cassidy stood near a small tree. She reached out and touched the smooth jade leaves and ran her fingers along the delicate branches. She looked up through the foliage to see the moon slip from behind a cloud and shed a golden light on the clearing.

In gold and jade, you will do what is right. She heard the words of Ng Mui and Wing Chun in her head. *We are with you, daughter. The time has come to fulfill your destiny!*

She gazed around the clearing, and her heart dropped when she didn't see the beautiful luminous spirits of the two Chinese warriors who were her ancestors—the women who told her that she couldn't run or hide from her destiny.

They promised I would have an ally, Cassidy thought. *Where is James now?*

Yet even though she wished for him to be at her side, there was a part of her that was glad that he wasn't. It was too dangerous. *There's nothing he could do, and I don't want him to get hurt.* She took a deep breath. "I'm glad he's not here," she whispered softly.

Cassidy thought about her friend Eliza. *I wish I could tell her how sorry I am that the fox demon attacked her.*

I wish I could tell her that I'm sorry that I wasn't always there for her. I wish I could thank her for being such a good friend. And for making me laugh so many times.

A twig snapped somewhere in the distance. She heard another sound—voices in the distance—but she couldn't tell how far away. *Am I hearing this because of my heightened senses or are they really close now?*

She strained to see through the darkness of night beyond the dimly lit clearing around the temple. *They're out there somewhere—Chiu Chi Lau, the three powerful hungry ghosts, and my father.*

❧ Chapter Thirty

"They're getting closer," Cassidy said to her grandfather as he walked up to her. "I can't see them yet, but I can hear them."

"Your extraordinary senses are a gift from our ancestors?" Grandfather Li asked.

"Yes," Cassidy said. "After I defeated the fox demon."

"Can you tell how far away they are?" he asked her.

"It's hard to tell. I can hear voices, but I can't make out what they're saying."

"I think the time has come, Mingmei," her grandfather said slowly. "We need to be ready when they get here."

"I don't expect you to fight, Grandfather," Cassidy said. "I don't want you to get hurt!"

"Mingmei, this is my battle, too," he said. "I wish I had stopped Chiu Chi Lau years ago when we were boys, but I realize now that it wouldn't have been possible."

What was her grandfather saying? "Do you mean that Chiu Chi Lau has always been stronger?"

"No," he said. "It's not what you're thinking. Lau and I studied with the same teacher. We were very competitive, and our skills were always closely matched."

"Then why do you say it wouldn't have been possible to stop him a long time ago?"

"Because of destiny, Mingmei," Grandfather Li said. "I think it's time to show you something. Please follow me."

Cassidy followed her grandfather into a pool of light under one of the brighter torches. He reached into one of his pockets and took out a piece of folded paper.

"These words are my own translation of the prophecy," he told her. "But I believe them to be accurate. The original document is a very brittle piece of paper, and the print is faded. It was to be kept in the wooden box along with the coins, but at some point it was lost. I found it again in a little known museum near the Shaolin Temple.

"The prophecy?" Cassidy asked. "I'm not sure I know what you —"

"Please just read this," he said. "It will all become clear to you."

So Cassidy took a deep breath and began reading, each word filling her with strength:

> *A daughter of light,*
> *Blood of Ng Mui and Yim Wing Chun,*
> *Will be born into the power of her ancestors,*
> *Born to finish the battles they began.*
> *In her fourteenth year her destiny will unfold:*
> *Through five gold coins, each death or strength.*
> *Her ancestors' enemies will seek her,*
> *The demons and ghosts will gather,*
> *But in gold and jade, she will find her gifts.*
> *And the veil of secrets will open to her.*

Tears stung Cassidy's eyes, but they weren't tears of sadness. *Why do I feel almost . . . hopeful?* And then suddenly she knew why. She had fought and defeated four of the five enemies, and each time she had received the gifts from her ancestors. She was truly a warrior!

But her eyes went back to the line: *Born to finish*

the battles they began. It wasn't finished, though. Not yet, anyway. The prophecy said each coin promised death or strength — nothing was certain. There was one more battle ahead of her, and this would be the most difficult. She had to save her father, her grandfather, and her ancestors. The prophecy had to be fulfilled! The last two lines made her believe that it was possible to succeed, but she had to wonder — at what cost?

Chapter Thirty-One

"They're very near," her grandfather said. "I'm afraid we don't have much time!" The urgency in his voice frightened Cassidy for a moment. She quickly refolded the slip of paper and tucked it into the silk pouch with the coins.

"We have the element of surprise on our side," Cassidy's grandfather said. "I think we should hide in the temple until they get here."

"I need to know the time," Cassidy said, straining to see the face of her watch in the darkness. In the flickering firelight Cassidy could see that it was already eleven thirty. "Only thirty minutes until midnight."

"Yes, I'm afraid that Lau has timed it just right," Grandfather Li said. "He believes that his plan is unfolding just as he anticipated. But he did not anticipate that he would find me here — alive and ready to stop him once and for all."

Cassidy heard the passion behind her grandfather's words, and she was afraid for him. She prayed that whatever lay ahead, her grandfather would not let his anger guide his fight. *The calm mind of a warrior,* Cassidy said to herself. *It's our only chance.*

Cassidy suddenly lifted her chin, listening intently.

"We are almost there," Chiu Chi Lau said. "You will see your daughter soon."

"This doesn't make any sense," Simon said. "First you said that Cassidy was in the hospital, and now you're bringing me up here! I want to see Cassidy now!"

"He's so worried," Cassidy told her grandfather. "I can hear him clearly."

"We must get ready." Her grandfather grabbed her by the arm and guided her toward the opening in the temple wall.

Now she heard a new voice, very faint, but a voice Cassidy could hear in her head — and in her heart: *We are with you, Mingmei. You cannot see us, but you can feel that we are with you. Hold fast to your calm mind and spirit. Remember, you are a warrior!*

Cassidy exhaled softly, and her grandfather did the same. Then she felt her grandfather's light touch on her arm. In the darkness she could just make out that he was pointing to a small crack between the large stones where a sliver of light sliced through.

She bent to peer through the crack. In the orange light of the flames that circled the ruins, she saw her teacher, his mouth stretched wide in what might have been some sort of demonic delight. Behind him were three large men dressed in black pants and shirts. *The demons disguised as men.* She shuddered as she imagined what kind of pure evil their human disguises hid.

Then she saw her father. One of the demons pushed him in front of Master Lau. His face was pale but defiant.

"I said I want to see Cassidy now!" he said between clenched teeth. "You told me that my daughter was hurt! Why are you doing this? Why did you bring me up here? I demand to see my daughter now!"

Master Lau laughed, and the shrill sound was like fingernails against a chalkboard to Cassidy's ears. "Oh, I'm afraid I've made a mistake." Master

Lau swept his arms to indicate the empty clearing. "It seems that your precious daughter is not here after all!"

"You said she'd be here!" her father said, his anger boiling over now. He rushed toward Master Lau, but one of the demons reached out and grabbed him. He yanked both arms sharply behind Simon's back.

"You are just as difficult as your father was," Master Lau complained. "He could have saved all of us this trouble years ago if he had just listened to me. It's a pity, really, that he's already dead. He would have been a much more satisfying sacrifice than you."

As Cassidy's father struggled to free himself from the demon who held him, Master Lau stepped forward. Cassidy frowned as she watched what was happening through the crack in the stone. Chiu Chi Lau reached toward her father's face slowly, gently even. Her father struggled to keep away from the *shifu's* hand.

What's he doing? Cassidy's mind screamed. Master Lau touched her father gently behind the ear the way a magician might just before removing an egg or a nickel at a child's birthday party. Cassidy watched in horror as her father's eyes went wide. Then they fluttered closed, and he slumped forward, a deadweight held upright by the powerful demon dressed in a man's clothes.

"Throw him over there," Master Lau said. "We need to get everything ready for the ritual. It's almost midnight!"

The demon lifted Simon's body in the air. Cassidy strained to free herself from her grandfather's strong arms. He had placed one hand over her mouth to stifle her scream just before her father fell to the hard-packed earth.

❧ Chapter Thirty-Two

"Listen," her grandfather whispered into her ear. "He isn't hurt. Only unconscious, that's all!"

Cassidy looked at her grandfather with questioning eyes, but he shook his head. "Let's find out how he plans to do this," he whispered. "Then we'll know the right moment to attack. It's the only way to save your father."

Cassidy's lungs felt seared from her muffled screams. She tried to control her breath and calm down so that she could think. *He's okay, my dad's okay,* she kept repeating to herself. *I have to be strong.*

She watched as Master Lau squatted in the clearing and opened up a duffel bag. He took out a large, dark sheet and spread it out on the ground, carefully smoothing out any wrinkles. Then he took several thick yellow candles and anchored the edges of the cloth with them.

"You should change now," he told the demons as he opened a vial of dark liquid. "If the girl has followed us, she should be here very soon."

The girl? Is he talking about me? Cassidy wondered.

"I can't believe that we even have to worry about her following us." He spat the words at one of the demons as he began lighting the candles. "You had the simple task of keeping your eyes on the girl and that arrogant boyfriend of hers, and somehow you manage to lose them both!"

He's talking about me and James! One of the demons had been watching us! But where's James now? He had said that he was going to some older section of Hong Kong, away from the tourist district, to look for Master Lau. Cassidy hoped with all her heart that James was back at the hotel. He would be wondering where Cassidy had gone, but he would have no idea where to look for her. *Please just let him stay at the hotel, where it's safe.*

"Thanks to you," Master Lau scolded one of the demons, "there's a good chance those two have managed to follow us. But I don't intend to let anything get in the way of my plan. So keep your eyes open for those two, and if you see them, kill the boy — but not the girl. After midnight, after the sacrifice, she'll simply disappear. But if you kill her, you'll ruin everything! Understand?"

All three of the demons nodded, and then Cassidy watched, sickeningly fascinated, as they began to transform. The first demon, the one that had been assigned the task of following Cassidy and James, spread his arms wide. As they lengthened he also grew taller. In the blink of an eye, he had morphed into a huge, vulturelike bird with sharp talons that gleamed like knives as they reflected the firelight. His beak was a glistening black and ended in a razor-sharp point. The demon's dark, feathered face scowled, and he opened his mouth wide and shrieked a loud *caw* that raised the hairs along the back of Cassidy's neck.

The second demon had changed, too. Cassidy froze in terror as she realized that this demon appeared to be a stone gargoyle — but with living, rippling flesh on his powerful arms and legs. His hideous head was frozen in a permanent stone grimace. He flexed his huge hands, and then closed them in again in two mighty stony fists. He reached out and smacked at a long thick limb on a nearby tree, and it snapped like twig. Cassidy heard her grandfather's sharp intake of breath as the tree limb crashed to the ground.

The third demon had the monstrous head of a

dragon on the muscled body of a man. He arched his neck and roared loudly. Flames shot from his open mouth—a blazing plume of orange and yellow fire that lit up the dark clearing. Cassidy caught the scent of sulfur hanging thick in the air.

Master Lau laughed. "Impressive, yes," he said. "But save it for the real fight if the girl shows up here. She is small, but she'll fight you to the death if she has to. I think the more likely scenario is that she'll come after me to save her father. Remember, you are here to protect me! Now one of you place our sacrifice on the altar."

The stone gargoyle demon placed the still body of Simon Chen in the center of the dark cloth as Master Lau directed. *He's so pale!* Cassidy realized. *Please let him be all right!*

Cassidy struggled to keep from being sick as she watched Master Lau place her father's hand across his chest. *Is this part of the ritual? Has it started?*

The three demons had returned to their lookout points along the perimeter of the clearing while Master Lau continued setting up his sacrificial altar.

"If only the girl knew how to really use the power of the coins, I could have spared her. We could have been partners!" he said, dripping oil onto each of the candles in succession. "But, as she told me one day in training, she only wants to do what is right." Master Lau sneered as he said the words.

Cassidy thought about the words of her ancestors — *in gold and jade, you will do what is right.* She shuddered, knowing this man she had once trusted had wanted her to become just as evil as he was.

The smell of rotting peaches permeated the air, and the candles began to sputter and sizzle. Master Lau looked up at the dark sky and then back down at Simon Chen, who lay in the middle of the dark cloth as quiet and still as death.

"I think it's time," Master Lau said. He returned to his duffel bag and reached in.

"Now! Let's strike now!" Cassidy whispered to her grandfather. She didn't want to see what Chiu Chi Lau was about to bring out of the bag. Neither did her grandfather. In one fluid motion Li Chen and Cassidy Chen burst through the opening between the ruined temple walls and landed in strike position on the hard-packed earth.

Before she could even blink, the bird demon was upon her.

❧ *Chapter Thirty-Three*

Cassidy threw all her weight against the muscled chest of the bird demon and began to pummel it. The bird swatted her with its powerful wing, and she went spinning backward and fell in a heap beneath a tree. Instantly, she was on her feet again, and this time the bird demon came after her with its talons ready to rip her apart. She heard Master Lau shriek, "No! You can't kill her!"

The bird demon paused long enough to give Cassidy the advantage. She leaped into the air and kicked the creature in the middle of the chest. A ragged caw escaped its beak just before it fell with a solid thud.

Cassidy glanced around to see that her grandfather and the stone gargoyle were circling each other. Then her grandfather rushed in and delivered a powerful punch that struck the demon just under its square jaw. The gargoyle's large head snapped back with the blow, and he emitted a groan that sounded like two boulders scraping against one another.

Master Lau stood near the edge of the dark cloth where Cassidy's father lay, watching the battle in confused fascination. *Of course!* He didn't know her grandfather was alive. He thought her grandfather had drowned years ago. Cassidy wondered how Master Lau felt about seeing his old enemy from long ago. *Maybe he thinks he's seeing a ghost.*

But there was no more time to observe her old teacher. The bird demon sprang forward and began slashing the air with its talons. Again, Master Lau screamed at him, "No! Remember that you can't kill her! I want those coins, you fool!"

But it seemed that this time the bird demon wasn't listening to the man who had allowed its early escape from the underworld. The demon flashed its burning eyes at Cassidy, and she knew that it was acting on its own now. If Master Lau had been able to control the demons before, now everything had changed—now the bird demon was angry, and Cassidy knew that it meant to kill her.

She heard the fiery roar of the dragon demon from the other side of the clearing and glanced quickly toward the noise. The creature moaned and tossed its heavy head back and forth as if it were in pain. Then she saw why.

James! James delivered a series of three quick and heavy blows to the back of the creature's neck. The demon dropped to the ground, writhing as it tried to roll away from its surprise attacker.

Cassidy had no time to think. She blocked the talons of the bird and then spun around and kicked hard. The bird demon tried to right itself but lost its balance and fell again, its caws turning into angry shrieks as it struggled to get to its feet.

The dragon demon was upright once more and began closing in on James. Cassidy watched as James moved into strike position and prepared for the next attack. A movement caught Cassidy's eye, and she froze when she saw what was about to happen.

She began to scream, "*James, behind you!*" but it was too late. The stone gargoyle hit James in the center of the back with its large granite fist.

Cassidy watched, sickened, as James's beautiful face contorted with pain and fear—almost in slow motion, it seemed to Cassidy. His head tilted back, and he fell to his knees. And then in one final graceful motion he fell forward and lay still.

"No!" Cassidy screamed as she ran toward James. One minute her feet were pounding the hard earth, and the next minute she was being lifted off the ground. She twisted around to see that the bird demon had caught her in its talons and had taken off into the air.

"Let me go!" she screamed, twisting and fighting, but the bird's grip was strong. She looked down at the scene below and saw her grandfather leap to the top of a stone wall. Below him the gargoyle pounded the wall with its fists. *He's going to fall! The demon is knocking down the wall!* Cassidy realized.

But in one fluid movement her grandfather leaped from the wall and came down hard on the stone gargoyle. The demon began to waver as it tried to regain its balance. And that's when Li Chen struck. He hit the gargoyle from behind and plowed him into the stone wall.

It was the sound of two planets colliding, and from her position above it all, Cassidy watched the wall begin to tumble down over the gargoyle. One large stone landed square on the demon's head and cracked it down the middle.

Ancient dust rose in a gray cloud above the destruction. Her grandfather was breathing hard, but Cassidy could see that he was okay as he prepared to fight the dragon demon, who had now started to circle him.

I have to get down there! Cassidy screamed inside. *I have to get away from this stupid bird demon!* She could see James lying unmoving where he fell. *Please don't let him be hurt! He was only trying to help me! Please don't let him be . . .* but she couldn't even think the words.

She saw Master Lau pacing around her father's still figure, watching the battle rage all around him but standing vigil, as if to protect his precious prey.

My father! I have to stop this now! Before midnight! Cassidy felt the bird demon's talons grip her shoulders even tighter. She winced as the sharp points sunk into her skin.

She reached up with both hands and grabbed the bird by its legs. Its talons dug in even deeper, and she felt warm liquid ooze down her back. *I'm bleeding,* she realized. But she continued fighting, attempting to twist her way out of the bird's grip.

Suddenly the strings of the silk coin pouch around her waist felt loose. In her struggle to get free from the bird demon, the thin ties on the pouch had either broken or started to untie. The heavy coins inside were pulling the silk pouch free.

The pouch fell away from her and hurtled toward the ground like a colorful broken kite. She looked down in time to see the cloth rip open as it hit the earth. The five gold coins spilled out on the dark ground and gleamed in the orange glow of the torches.

Master Lau rushed to the coins but suddenly stopped as if he had slammed into an invisible barrier. His hands stretched toward the coins and his fingers quivered—but the protective magic in them kept him away. Cassidy knew that he couldn't put his hands on them—not yet, anyway.

From somewhere down the mountain, Cassidy heard drums banging, bells ringing, and the thunderous roar of fireworks. Off in the distance she saw bonfires beginning to burn.

It's midnight! This is it! She twisted the bird demon's legs and at the same time, she scissored through the air, moving her legs quickly back and forth in order to bring down the demon. The demon, in order to stay aloft, beat the air with its powerful wings. But Cassidy was stronger, and she began to pull the bird demon back down to the clearing.

Down on the ground the demon reached out to bite her with its needlesharp beak, but Cassidy kicked it hard, sending it spiraling back in a furious whirl of glistening black feathers. It came at her once more, but Cassidy was ready. This time she took two gliding steps and then flew through the air to meet the bird demon several feet above the ground. She struck it again and again in its soft neck. It tried to caw, and then to shriek, but nothing came out except a sickening gurgle as it attempted to get away from Cassidy. She pulled the bird back down to the ground hard, and the outstretched wings hit the earth first. Cassidy heard the crunch of thin bones as the broken wings folded in for good on the bird demon.

Taking a deep breath, Cassidy realized that there was only one demon left. The dragon had cornered her grandfather against the stone wall. Each breath was a fiery torch that, so far, he had been able to dodge. But the stone wall behind him was blackened with soot and ashes. Each time her grandfather attempted to rush forward and strike, the dragon demon would bellow and her grandfather would be forced to retreat.

I'll distract the demon! Cassidy thought. *Then Grandfather can get away!* "No-o-o-o-o!" she screamed, and advanced toward the dragon, ready to quickly roll to the side if she saw flames.

The dragon turned and looked toward Cassidy, allowing her grandfather a chance to move out of the demon's path. The dragon advanced, ready to burn Cassidy to a crisp. Just then Cassidy heard a voice that chilled her to the marrow. "Don't harm the girl! I have a job for you that you'll like. Over here! If you want to kill the boy, then be my guest!"

Both Cassidy and the dragon demon stopped and looked toward Master Lau, who now kneeled at James's side with his hand on his forehead.

"I'm afraid this boy feels a little cold," he said. "I think he may be ill. Perhaps he needs a bit of . . . warming up? Come take care of this for me, and then we'll have the sacrifice. You must be very hungry. And just think! Now all those lovely spirits will be just for you!"

The dragon demon seemed to be breathing hard as it considered what Master Lau was saying. Cassidy saw short wisps of dark smoke escape its nostrils as it took several ragged breaths. She prayed that the demon had been weakened from its fight with her grandfather. But in one powerful leap, the dragon demon stood over James.

Cassidy began to dart toward the creature that was half dragon, half man, but her grandfather reached out and dragged her back to him. "I have to stop him," she screamed, struggling to free herself from her grandfather's powerful grip. "I can't let him do this to James!"

"You can't, Mingmei! He'll kill you! I'm afraid it may already be too late for James," her grandfather said softly as he held her close.

Cassidy moaned as she buried her head against her grandfather's shoulder. She shut her eyes tightly just before she heard the awful roar of a thousand fires.

❧ Chapter Thirty-Four

"I will stop you!" Cassidy screamed as she whirled away from her grandfather and raced toward the creature. The dragon demon turned and faced Cassidy. She couldn't bring herself to look down at James—she didn't want to know how badly he was burned.

She had one thing on her mind now. To kill the dragon demon and send the vile creature back to the underworld, where it belonged. The thing shook its massive head and bellowed up to the sky. The roar rocked the surrounding trees, making them tremble, and Cassidy knew that it was getting ready to attack. The massive arms of the dragon demon spread wide as it inhaled deeply.

"I will stop you!" Cassidy cried again as she faced the dragon, no more than twenty feet away now. Her chest was heaving, and she knew that she needed to call upon her warrior's calm mind to get her through this last fight.

For only a moment she closed her eyes, and in that instant she pictured the tranquil pool of water. But this time it was frozen over. An icy mist blew across the glistening pond, and sharp and deadly icicles hung from the trees that surrounded the peaceful, now frozen water.

Take a deep breath, my daughter, and then use it, Cassidy heard her ancestors' voices say. *Use it?* she wondered. She knew the importance of controlling her breath and how it could calm her when her mind raced, but how was she supposed to use it?

Cassidy opened her eyes and saw that the dragon had advanced another few feet. It tossed its head back, and Cassidy knew what was coming. She breathed in and felt an unnatural chill deep in her lungs. In one long breath she exhaled as she spoke the powerful words again: "I will stop you!"

The dragon's fire met Cassidy's icy breath in the space between the two of them. Cassidy could hardly believe what she was seeing as the orange and red flames crystallized in midair and formed daggerlike icicles. Like shattering glass, the frozen fire fell to the ground between them.

In a blindingly fast move Cassidy ran in and struck the dragon demon hard. The monster fell back, and Cassidy was on it in an instant. It tried to roll away from her, but her strikes were so hard and furious that it didn't get far.

The mound of fiery icicles shifted, and a particularly long one slid toward Cassidy's foot. She reached down and picked up the sharp dagger of fire and ice. In one fluid move she raised it above her head and then plunged it into the chest of the dragon demon, pinning it to the ground. Its eyes widened as the demon looked up at Cassidy and then at the weapon, as if it was surprised to find it there in its chest. It coughed once, a dark puff of ashes, and then became still.

On the other side of the clearing, at the edge of the dark cloth where her father lay, Cassidy saw that her grandfather and Master Lau were circling each other as if they were practicing *chi sau*.

Sticking hands. She remembered Master Lau's words from when he was someone she trusted. Feel your enemy's commitment to fight. *When you understand your enemy's commitment, then you will know when and how to strike!*

Her grandfather was very good, each step sure and confident. Cassidy was absolutely certain of his commitment to fight. He was fighting for the life of his son. He was fighting for the lives of all his loved ones. He had to stop this man, his former friend from so many years ago. But Master Lau's commitment was equally strong and determined.

Cassidy moved in closer, ready to strike, to assist her grandfather at the right moment. Continuing to circle, never taking his eyes from Li Chen, Master Lau was still able to notice that Cassidy was coming near.

"Should I play with him, Cassidy?" Master Lau asked in his dead-as-dust voice. "Or should I do this the quick way?"

The man's mocking tone angered Cassidy. She started to run toward them, but her grandfather's words stopped her. "No, Mingmei," he said firmly. "This is my fight now. I wish I could have stopped this man fifty years ago, but it wasn't possible then."

Master Lau laughed. "*You* should have stopped *me*? That's such a joke! You were too busy running away, remember? You were pretending to be dead!"

"Only to protect my family from you!" her grandfather said to him. "I never left them. I've watched over them for years. I've watched you, too, Chiu Chi Lau. For years." Cassidy noticed a flash of emotion cross Lau's face. *Surprise? Anger?* But just as quickly, his face returned to its neutral state, giving away nothing.

And then suddenly, Master Lau began to laugh again, an evil, dark sound that seemed to come from the bottom of a grave. "Li Chen, do you realize that you brought all of this on yourself?"

"No," Cassidy's grandfather said calmly. "It's your greed that brought you here. You wanted the coins from the first moment you saw them. You saw an evil purpose in the coins, and you've hungered to own them ever since."

Cassidy could see her grandfather's chest rise and fall in even breaths as he spoke. She was in awe at the control her grandfather had.

But if Li Chen's words of truth disturbed Chiu Chi Lau in any way, his face didn't show it. "We could have worked together as partners if you'd only listened to me," he said disdainfully. "You owned the coins, but I had the knowledge and the power to use them. The dark magic would have allowed us to use the power to get whatever we wanted! Fame, riches, even immortality. All of it would have been ours! Instead what do you do? You put the coins in the hands of your granddaughter, a fourteen-year-old girl! I'm afraid that whatever happens now is because of you."

At that moment Cassidy saw the briefest flicker of emotion in her grandfather's eyes. *Does he feel guilty about giving me the coins? Does he feel that he could have protected me from having to fulfill this destiny somehow?*

Cassidy wanted to scream, "Don't listen to

him! You did the right thing—the only thing!" but there was no time for words. In the split second that Cassidy's grandfather wavered, his old-friend-turned-enemy struck. Chiu Chi Lau attacked with a quick circle to the left, coming around with a kick that he put all his power into, landing it squarely in the center of her grandfather's chest. Cassidy gasped as Li Chen attempted to block and dodge. But he was a second too late, and she heard the air rush from her grandfather's lungs.

Chapter Thirty-Five

Cassidy's hands flew to her mouth. She expected to see her grandfather fall. But to her utter amazement he seemed to absorb the powerful blow instead of resisting it. He stumbled back several steps and then quickly regained his balance.

Chiu Chi Lau, however, was so certain that the blow had dropped Li Chen for good that he turned from Li Chen to sneer at Cassidy, an arrogant and pleased expression on his face.

From what seemed like a lifetime ago, the words of Master Lau came to Cassidy now. She remembered the day he had impressed them all by teaching them tiger-style kung fu: *When springing forward to attack,* he had instructed, *do not hesitate, do not question. Once the tiger makes the decision to attack, his purpose is simple: to kill.*

Cassidy ran, then gracefully leaped from the ground straight up to the top of the temple wall. She landed softly but solidly on the ancient stones. She gazed down at the man who would never be her teacher again. He moved into strike position, but at the same time he watched her with both amazement and fear on his face. Cassidy took a deep breath, allowing the love of her ancestors to fill her whole body.

We are all with you, said the mingled voices of her great-grandmother Fiona, her Chinese ancestors Ng Mui and Wing Chun, and others she didn't recognize. Cassidy understood that all the ancestors from both sides of her family—Irish and Chinese—had now come together to give her unmatched strength and power. If she failed, they would all be devoured.

And then she attacked. In one perfect leap she rose off the stone wall, flew through the air, and landed soundlessly, effortlessly, in front of Chiu Chi Lau, her hands expertly poised in the strike position of the crane. The unexpected force of her first blow took her former teacher by total surprise and spun him around.

Cassidy started to move in for a final, deadly

blow, but then stopped when she saw her grandfather — a grim determination on his face. As Lau spun dizzily, Li Chen raced toward him, leaped up as if he might be running through the air, and then kicked with a force that propelled Chiu Chi Lau toward the stone wall of the temple.

Cassidy and her grandfather watched Master Lau slam hard against the wall and then slide down into the dust like a broken puppet. His eyes stared straight up into the midnight sky, a sky illuminated with a thousand stars, but he didn't blink. Cassidy watched in horror as a dark spirit rose from Master Lau's chest and lingered above his body for a moment. It then fell back down to the ground like an oily stain before soaking into the dust.

Even before the spirit of Chiu Chi Lau vanished completely, Cassidy was at her father's side, kneeling on the dark cloth that would have been the sacrificial altar. His face was pale, but she was relieved to see the steady rise and fall of his chest. "He's going to be fine, Mingmei," her grandfather assured her as he knelt beside her. He placed his hand over his son's. "Let me attend to him."

"Crane Girl." The voice was hoarse and almost inaudible, but Cassidy heard it. She turned toward James. He was trying to sit up, but she could see that he was very weak. She ran to him and knelt at his side. His beautiful face was red and blistered. His too-long but wonderful dark hair had been singed along one side. And Cassidy saw that his sweatshirt was pocked with dark, smoky burns.

"I thought you'd be . . ." But she couldn't form the words.

"There was a light," James whispered hoarsely. "It . . . I think it protected me when the dragon . . ."

"Don't talk, James," Cassidy said, her voice thick with tears that she fought to hold back. "Don't move. You're . . . you're going to be all right. I'll help you."

But even as Cassidy spoke, she realized that she didn't know how she could help him. Her grandfather came to Cassidy's side and felt James's pulse.

"He's very weak," he whispered into Cassidy's ear. "The stone gargoyle hit him hard, Mingmei."

James tried again to speak, but his voice was no more than a whispery scratch now. Cassidy leaned in closer to hear him. "Crane Girl," he said, and Cassidy saw that he was attempting to smile. "You're so brave! I . . . I saw you fly!" The effort of the words was too much, and Cassidy's heart ached as she watched him lean back again, shutting his eyes.

"We have to do something!" she begged her grandfather. "I have to get help!"

Her grandfather shook his head and put his arm around Cassidy's shoulder. "Mingmei, there's no time to get help. He's hurt very badly." She looked at James as he tried to breathe. Each small breath seemed labored and empty of air.

"No," Cassidy said, tears falling freely down her face now. "No, I can't let this happen to him. It's all my fault! He never would have been hurt if I hadn't asked him to help me. I told him that he was my ally!"

Cassidy looked down at the ground through tear-blurred eyes. She noticed the shimmery fabric of red silk. *The silk pouch*, she realized, and remembered it falling from her waist when the bird demon flew into the air with her. Near the pouch were the gold coins scattered around on the ground, along with her passport and the folded paper copy of the prophecy that her grandfather had given her. *Would there be help from the coins now?* Cassidy dared to hope. Would there be a gift that would save her friend?

❧ Chapter Thirty-Six

Cassidy picked up the coins and felt their warmth, as she had after each battle with a demon. *All this destruction—this pain—because Master Lau wanted these coins for his own.* She wiped her eyes on her sleeve and examined the fifth coin. Around the outer edge of the coin were the hungry, open mouths of the ghosts—the dark, lost, starving, wandering souls who got one night a year to leave the underworld.

And like people, Cassidy realized, *some of the hungry ghosts were simply troublesome, while others were pure evil.*

But there was something different about the coin now, and as Cassidy ran her finger over the engraving she realized what it was. There was no center!

The middle of the coin — a perfect circle — had dropped out, leaving a hole large enough for her to pass her little finger through. "Look at this," she said, handing it to her grandfather. He studied the coin and frowned, puzzled.

Cassidy peered down at the dust where the coins had landed. She brushed her hand across the ground and then picked up something small and round. She rubbed it clean with her thumb and then showed it to her grandfather.

"I think it's another coin," she said. Immediately she remembered the hungry ghost at the window of the museum's research room and how he had asked about the sixth coin! She turned the small coin over in her hand. It was no more than a small round disk, and it had fit perfectly within the circle of the hungry ghost coin. It had been there all along — *a coin within a coin*, she realized now.

"This is very remarkable," her grandfather said. "I've read nothing about a sixth coin."

Unlike the five gold coins, this one was made of jade. Rather than an image of a demon, there were the delicate lines of a beautiful crane etched in the center of the small coin. How had she not been able to see this before? Was it like her destiny, hidden behind the veil until she had secured the fate of her ancestors?

James's breath was even more ragged now, and Cassidy saw that he seemed to be struggling to speak again. She had to find some way to help him. She clutched her fist tightly in frustration, and the small jade coin grew warm. She felt herself fill with the strength of her ancestors but realized that it did nothing to ease the ache in her heart as she sat in the dust next to her friend.

"The coin," she said to her grandfather. "I think the jade coin is my gift this time. The gift received for fulfilling the prophecy!"

"Yes, my granddaughter," he said. "I think you're right. The prophecy said that in gold and jade you would find your gifts."

Cassidy nodded. "I think it's giving me strength," she said. "I feel it. It's as if some kind of power is coursing through me. Do you think it could . . . could it help James? Do you think I could give it to him?"

She remembered James's words when he was helping her find out what the coins were all about: *What if they can't be taken—only given?* She looked at her grandfather, and it was as if he could read the question in her face. He nodded yes and then smiled.

Cassidy reached for James's hand and opened it. She placed the still-warm jade coin in his hand and wrapped his fingers around it. She closed her own hand over his, letting whatever strength or healing power she had flow through her and into him. And then her hand grew warm, and she saw a shimmering pair of hands cover her own. She looked up and saw a luminous spirit that she knew must be James's mother—beautiful and full of love for her son.

James's eyes fluttered opened and began to clear. Cassidy reached out and touched the burned skin on his face. Beneath her hands the skin began to heal, the angry red burns fading entirely away. His mother's spirit smiled at Cassidy and vanished.

Cassidy and her grandfather helped James as he attempted to sit up straighter. She saw that he winced with each movement. Placing her hand on his back, she supported him where he took the hard hit from the stone gargoyle demon. She felt his muscles strengthen beneath her palm. "You're going to be all right," she assured him softly. "But how did you know where to find me?"

"I found Lau," James explained. "Then I saw your father get in the car with him. I followed in a cab until they got to the mountain."

"I'm so sorry you got hurt, James," Cassidy said. "I never wanted anything to happen to you."

But James wasn't listening. "I saw her," he said to Cassidy, his eyes wide with wonder. "It was just for a minute, but I saw her. I saw my mother."

Cassidy nodded and smiled at him. "Yes, she was here, James. I saw her, too."

Once he moved into a better sitting position, James opened his hand and looked at the jade coin. He frowned, surprised to find it there.

"It's the sixth coin," Cassidy told him. "It's yours now."

Cassidy noticed that James's attention was drawn to other side of the clearing. She glanced over and watched her grandfather helping her father to his feet. She felt an immediate urge to rush over—but then stopped herself. Her own emotions at this reunion were almost overwhelming—she could only imagine what *they* were feeling. This was an amazing and important moment between the two of them. Father and son faced each other, and then embraced, their warm love for each other melting away all the lost years.

"Where's . . . where's Lau?" James asked. Cassidy was relieved to hear that James's voice sounded stronger. "What happened to him?"

Cassidy pointed over to the stone wall, where she had watched her once-beloved teacher fall into the dust and die. But he wasn't there! She squinted and looked again. Could her eyes be playing tricks on her? But no—he was really gone!

Chapter Thirty-Seven

Cassidy rushed over to the stone temple wall. Her sudden movement made her grandfather turn toward her. That's when he also noticed that Chiu Chi Lau's body was no longer lying like a broken toy in the dust.

Together they examined the area next to the wall where they had seen him fall. There were no footprints except their own. The bodies of the three demons had also disappeared.

"What do you think happened?" Cassidy asked her grandfather. "Where did he go?"

"I think it's possible that Chiu Chi Lau was so deeply involved in dark magic that he's joined the underworld as a demon," he said. "Perhaps his body has ceased to exist so that his spirit could take on the supernatural aspect of a demon. Think of the demons you've encountered, Mingmei—winged snakes, plague ghosts, fox demons, and—"

Cassidy finished the sentence for him. "And the darkness within. The dark half inside me—inside all of us," she said.

"Yes," her grandfather said. "Exactly. Those thoughts, wishes, and desires are within all of us. But we don't have to let them control us, like Chiu Chi Lau did."

"He used the hungry demons of the fifth coin to try to achieve his evil goals," Cassidy said. "So in a way, he *became* the fifth demon I'd been expecting— because of his obsessions and dark magic."

"I'm afraid so, Mingmei."

Cassidy's father came and stood between her and her grandfather. He couldn't seem to stop looking at his father with wonder. "What happened up here?" He was still groggy and confused, and his speech slightly slurred. "Master Lau told me there'd been an accident. He said you were in the hospital. He had three men with him. But instead he brought me here—why? I knew something was wrong. He wouldn't tell me anything."

Cassidy looked at her grandfather. *How to even begin!* she wondered. Then her grandfather put his arm around his son.

"Simon," he said, "I am the luckiest man alive today. I've been given the gift of time—time to be with my family again, and time to explain everything when we get back home."

Far below the mountain the twinkling lights of Hong Kong glittered. Cassidy thought that they seemed as far away as the stars above them; as far away as her mother and her best friend Eliza; as far away as Luis, who was probably sleeping soundly in the hotel, dreaming of the Wing Chun tournament that would soon begin.

But will it? Cassidy wondered. *Without Master Lau, will the tournament go on?* She doubted it and wondered how Master Lau's disappearance would be explained. *I'm not even going to think about that now,* she decided. *I'm just happy to be alive and to be with my family and . . . and with James.*

Cassidy helped James to his feet. For a moment Cassidy, James, her father, and her grandfather stood shoulder to shoulder on top of the mountain. Their faces glowed in the fires from the torchlight that burned in memory of the fallen monks. The small group was silent as they looked out over the horizon, where the palest orange light of the rising sun was beginning to appear.

Cassidy sensed the presence of someone else standing nearby. She turned to see dozens, or maybe even hundreds, of her ancestors gathering around.

She saw Ng Mui, Wing Chun, her great-grandmother Fiona, and now thousands of other loving faces, smiling at her, filling her with their love.

"*Thank you, Mingmei,*" Ng Mui said in a strong clear voice. Wing Chun stood next to Ng Mui, dazzling in her apricot silk.

"*You are our warrior princess, Mingmei,*" Wing Chun said. "*We are very proud of you. Because of you we are here.*"

"And because of *you*," Cassidy said, "I am here."

"Who are they?" Simon asked in confusion. "Who are all these people? Am I seeing things?"

Dad can see them, too?

"My guess is that these are our ancestors, Simon." Cassidy's grandfather gazed at the throng of ethereal beings that surrounded them now. The spirit of a beautiful woman raised a radiant hand in a small gesture, almost a shy wave. The rising sun dusted her fingertips with a warm glow as she smiled at Li Chen.

"That's your grandmother," Grandfather Li said to Cassidy, his voice thick with emotion. He lifted his own hand to wave back to her and then kissed his fingertips. "This is truly a gift," he said.

"You can see them, too, Grandfather?" Cassidy said in absolute amazement. She turned to James. "And you?"

James nodded and pointed toward his mother, who smiled at him and then nodded to Cassidy. The look on her face was radiant and beautiful. She smiled at James with no sadness and no regrets. Cassidy saw James take a deep breath and then smile. Cassidy hoped that seeing his mother this one last time would help James with the healing process.

"They can *see* you! All of you!" Cassidy said to the spirits, her voice trembling. "This . . . this is the best gift ever." Cassidy felt honored and deeply grateful to the spirits for revealing themselves to her father, her grandfather, and to James.

"*No, it is we who are grateful to all of you,*" said Ng Mui. "*You have fulfilled the prophecy. You came together to put an end to a terribly evil plan. And we come together now to thank you.*"

As the morning sun inched higher over the horizon the brilliant, luminous spirits began to fade. For several minutes after the last spirit disappeared, the four of them continued to stand in awestruck silence, holding on to the images of their loved ones for as long as possible. Cassidy knew that this appearance had been a true gift for all of them and something that none of them would ever forget.

At last, Grandfather Li spoke. "I believe it's

time to leave the mountain. Do you feel well enough, Simon?"

Cassidy's father nodded. Cassidy could see that he was stronger. The color had returned to his face. Even though he still looked confused about everything that had happened, she knew that he was going to be okay.

"And what about you?" Grandfather Li asked James.

"I'm fine. In fact, I feel great. I feel like I could race down the mountain."

"Do you think you could beat me?" Cassidy teased him.

James smiled as he thought about it. "Actually, probably not," he admitted reluctantly. Then he grinned. "Maybe tomorrow, but not today."

Together they started down the narrow, flower-lined path that would take them back to the city. Cassidy and James followed behind her grandfather and her father. She was thrilled as she watched the two of them ahead of her. She shook her head in amazement when she realized how similar their walks were, arms swinging wide and slightly forward, shoulders slightly sloped, father and son.

As she watched her father and grandfather, James reached out to take Cassidy's hand. Her heart soared. *I'm holding hands with James Tang.* After a moment she felt him slip the coin into her palm.

She stopped on the path and gazed down at the jade coin etched with the beautiful crane, and then looked back up at James.

"It's really yours," he said. "You saved my life with it, but it's your coin."

"No," she said, giving the coin back to him. "We did this together. The coin is yours now."

James laughed, and the sound was like music to Cassidy's ears. "So does this mean that I'm part of your destiny, Crane Girl?"

Cassidy's heart beat a little faster, and she smiled. "James, you have been from the start. You just didn't know it."

For a moment James looked as if he didn't know what to say. "Yeah, I guess I have been all along," he said finally. "So how come it took me so long to figure that out?"

Cassidy smiled. "That's easy. Because all you could see was a fourteen-year-old girl with a huge crush on you."

James laughed and nodded slightly. "Yeah, I guess you're right." His dark eyes still twinkled but grew more serious. "What do I see now?"

"Only you can answer that," she said softly.

"You're right," James said. "And I really like what I see. Not a kid, but a beautiful green-eyed warrior."

Cassidy smiled at James, feeling confident

and strong. She took in a deep breath and then began running ahead on the trail in front of James, passing her father and her grandfather.

The early morning sun turned the pale flowers that edged the narrow green path a golden yellow. "I am *so* much more than just a beautiful green-eyed warrior, James Tang!" she called back to him.

Cassidy held her arms out wide and shouted for all of Hong Kong, for all of the world to hear. "I am Mingmei—the kung fu princess!"